ROBYN SMYTHE

FALLON

The Legacy Series:

Part Four – 'Secret Agent Man'

Grosvenor House
Publishing Limited

The right of Robyn Smythe to be identified as the author of this
work has been asserted in accordance with Section 78
of the Copyright, Designs and Patents Act 1988

The book cover is copyright to Robyn Smythe
Cover design by Brian Jones

This book is published by
Grosvenor House Publishing Ltd
Link House
140 The Broadway, Tolworth, Surrey, KT6 7HT.
www.grosvenorhousepublishing.co.uk

This book is a work of fiction. Any resemblance to
people or events, past or present, is purely coincidental.

A CIP record for this book
is available from the British Library

Paperback ISBN 978-1-83615-500-3
eBook ISBN 978-1-83615-501-0

This book is dedicated to Clarky.
Both my friend and colleague,
who's sideways look at life
has helped me through some of
life's challenges.

I would also like a special mention to the staff of the
New Lanark Mill hotel for their professionalism
and care they showed my wife and I during
our numerous visits.

Rx

Table of Contents

Prologue

'*The Office of Special Projects was founded in 1906 after a memo from the then Prime Minister, Henry Campbell-Bannerman, was circulated in the Home Office, urging the formation of an Intelligence Section that was under the control of the Government. It was to be an elite group, so secret, that only the PM and the Home Secretary knew of its existence. Under the command of colonel John Forrester, it operated out of Egypt during the Great War (1914 – 18) with many successes, most of which attributed to other agencies.*

Operatives were recruited from the armed services and although their military training went along way, to each one gaining the coveted 'K' letter and number, other specialist training was given, still covered under the official secrets act.

One of the successes was the stopping of 'Operation Phoenix,' a privately funded attempt to raise a Bedouin army to fight against the Allies. It was later found out that French Industrialist, Alexandre Falcone, was behind

'Phoenix.' Three years after the end of the war, Falcone was tracked down to his private island and eliminated by a joint OSP and American Secret Intelligence Service operation, sanctioned by both governments at the highest levels.

One of the OSP operatives, Jonathan Fallon, was later awarded the George Cross, at an unofficial ceremony in Buckingham Palace and officially retired from active service. colonel Forrester continued as head of OSP secretively watching the world change from his office somewhere in the capital. SIS disappeared being replaced by the OSS (Office of Strategic Services) by President Roosevelt, and Churchill, at the beginning of the Second World War, founded the Special Operations Executive, or SOE. Both these institutions would go on to operate with great success during the conflict while the OSP, who would quietly wait in the wings, as it were, to be called upon again.

Once hostilities had ended in 1945, a new threat appeared on the horizon in the form of the Soviet Union, a one-time ally and now emerging superpower. New agencies evolved from the conflict, CIA, MI6, and MI5, to deal with the new red menace while, in the shadows, OSP sat back and watched. Training continued. Intelligence was gathered.

Forrester also decided to use a media company as a cover for his government work and the 'Swinton Newspaper Group' allowing his operatives to travel the globe under the umbrella of being journalists without raising suspicion. Relationships cultivated.

In late 1950, Forrester passed away of a heart attack peacefully at his London home. A column in the Times obituaries mentioned his military service but, under a red notice from the Government, omitted his work at the OSP.

The control of OSP was taken over, firstly, by a minister from the Home Office and then it was considered necessary to put it under military control because of the worsening situation with the Russians.

Even with much consternation from ministers, the Office of Special Projects went under the command of the Joint Chiefs of Staff, who used 'K-Section' for some off the book's operations, or black ops, to use the more modern coin of phrase, some very dubious indeed.

Because of these nefarious missions, the OSP became known as 'The Dirty Tricks' squad. It was tarnished with this moniker until the late nineties when a new commander was appointed and the OSP broke free of the Joint Chiefs shackles. The OSP's saviour was colonel James Scott.

An experienced career officer with extensive covert training with the Special Air Service and a short spell with the American Special Forces in Vietnam. During the next decade, Scott came in hard with a broom, throwing out some of the antiquated practices, giving operatives free reign on equipment choice and more flexible conditions.

1 – *Heart Not in It*

Eagleton golf club and resort was built in the late Nineties by a tech billionaire who had since faded into obscurity. Designed by the former golf professional Douglas Swinton, who had found brief fame on the America US PGA Tour, winning a few of the minor titles. It was your typical eighteen-hole course with a mixture of sand traps, trees, and vegetation hazards to add to the golfer's excitement. An average round would take the average person around three hours to complete.

The Eagleton club house doubled as both a locker room and hotel, costing around twelve hundred pounds annually for membership. For that, a member would get exclusive access to the leisure facilities of the hotel which included a spa, massage, gym, and swimming pool.

Entering the reception area was like heading back in time to an age of opulence. No expense had been spared in creating this showcase mixture of finance and comfort. Leather sofas were dotted around the room, tables sat in between them, their position slightly off centre to add a sense of intrigue. A piano sat at the back of the room, the instrument silently begging someone to pluck up the courage and sit down to tinkle its ivories.

Robert Jenkins appeared from the locker room; his golf bag slung across his shoulders. He paused at the bottom of the steps that shot upwards to the road above. He was getting too old for this and rolled his eyes. Take up a past time they said. You will enjoy it, they said. Something to do in your retirement, they said. He cursed under his breath before inhaling deeply. His mind made up, he started to scale the slope in front of him like an experienced climber trying the side of a mountain.

The spikes on the soles of his shoes clicked with each step, making him sound like an amateur tap dancer in need of some much-needed practice, did little to aid in gripping the already wet concrete that the steps were constructed from.

The steps, allowed for very little '*wiggle*' room never mind a man in the latter part of his life carrying a heavy bag containing his weapons of choice across his back. He now knew how a pack mule felt transporting goods up those jungle paths he had seen in a recent television documentary about the last war in Burma.

Eventually, his tired and withered frame peaked over the crest of the stairs. Breathless, he hauled himself the finally few steps before unstrapping his bag, propping it up against the wrought iron fence that ran along the front of the entrance to the clubhouse. He bent over, placing his hands upon his thighs, sweat cascading down his face like a river of exertion.

The sound of a car's engine made him look up, just in time to see a black Mercedes saloon stop across from him. There was the faint sound of humming, like a contented honeybee, as the window nearest to him went down. A man's face appeared. The sight of it made Jenkins' blood run cold. He recognised the man as Otto Werner, a former associate of his from an earlier life. A life that he had long since forgotten, relegating it to his past. Werner flicked his fingers, summoning him.

Like an obedient lamb, Jenkins went slowly across and stood beside the car. Werner leaned over the back of his chair, rummaged for a moment and then brought out a bottle of water. He handed the bottle to Jenkins. There was nothing striking about the contents, simply a sample of H_2O. It was the label that stuck out. It was a cartoon depiction of a robin redbreast with the name '*Petirrojo Water Company*' in bold letter underneath.

"Are you still playing with Eric Fuller?" Snarled Werner.

Jenkins nodded sheepishly.

"Good. Your instructions are to give him this halfway round...." Werner's expression changed as a contented smile appeared. ".... the effects will be interesting, shall we say."

Jenkins' face changed to one of shock as he realised to what Werner was implying. "Why am I doing this to him?"

"My superiors are telling me he's getting too close."

Jenkins reluctantly nodded his compliance.

"Let's just say his heart won't be in it." Werner hissed, making him sound like a tyre with a leak. "Failure to comply will result in dire consequences for you, Herr Jenkins." Werner warned menacingly as the window went slowly back up. The engine gunned and then the saloon sped off leaving Jenkins alone with the bottle of water and his thoughts.

At 1530 precisely, Eric Fuller appeared on the first tee, a par four. Jenkins was a few minutes behind. They nodded and shook hands. They spoke for a moment, deciding who would tee-off first, therefore, beginning their contest, like two gladiators of olden times. They decided that Fuller would have the honour. He went across to his bag, unzipped a pocket in the side of it, took out a plastic tee and a white dimpled ball with a black tick prominent on it.

He strode up to the marker, put his ball on top of the tee, placing them between his first two fingers, he bent at the waist and pushed the tee into the soft earth. He returned to his bag, pulled out his large headed driver, then returned to the tee, taking up position on the left-hand side of the tee / ball combination.

He took up his stance, feet hip width apart, his body a club length away from the target. He moved his head from side to side until his neck clicked. Wiggled his hips a little and he was ready. He took a step back and did a couple of practice swings before stepping back in to address the ball once more. His arms tensed.

His head turned, his grey blue eyes looking down the fairway, his mind picturing his ball soaring off into the sky before landing onto the greener than green lush fairway and scuttling along before coming to rest a few hundred yards from where it had been launched.

Like Jenkins, Fuller's age limited his range of movement, but he had adapted his game accordingly. Sure, his swing would make a golfing coach cringe or turnover in his grave, but he did not care. It worked for him. The club went backwards, stopped just below his shoulders before he used his arms, hips, and the rest of his body to drive the weapon forward. The head making a satisfying pinging sound as it collided at speed with ball, firing it forwards at great velocity.

Fuller's follow-through finished just below his shoulders. His head turning in unison with the stroke, pausing at the top of the follow-through to watch the projectile power away. A smile appearing on his battle-hardened features. Jenkins was carbon copy of Fuller, thumping the ball skywards as hard as he could. They collected their bags, instantly regretting not hiring either a buggy or trolleys. They set off after their balls making small talk as golfers do. Bouncing from one subject to another, like their balls along the fairway.

They found Jenkins' ball first. Down went the bag onto the ground. Jenkins swore under his breath as he reached down to pull it upright, fishing out an iron and then turning his attention to the ball. He had found a decent lie and approached it like a predator stalking his prey. He did not mess about, like he did with his initial drive, he glance towards his target, the flag on the green fluttering away in the wind and took his shot. A large divot of grass launched into the air plopping to the ground a few feet in front of him.

The ball arced and bounced three times before rolling to a standstill a few inches from the safety of the green. Fuller walked up and found his ball in some light rough. He decided to use an angled wedge and hacked at it with all his strength. The ball shot from the club head heading towards the green, but he had given it too much power, and it overshot, coming to rest a few feet off the surface teetering on the edge of a sand trap, or bunker as they call it in Britain.

Both men took three more strokes to hole out but were satisfied with the result. And this how it continued until they reached the turn, or homeward holes. Number ten was a simple par three. Both managed to reach the green in one but had varied success. Fuller was fifteen feet away from the hole whilst Jenkins was six from the comfort of the cup. They both holed out for a welcome birdie.

Fuller picked his ball out of the hole and walked over to his bag, reached down to one of the side pockets, searched inside for a moment and then stood up, his hands on his hips, clearly aggravated about something.

"Is everything okay, Eric?" Inquired Jenkins.

"No, damn it!" Replied Fuller. "My throat is drier than the Sahara, and I've forgotten to bring some bloody water!" He threw his arms up in frustration. The outburst stunned Jenkins. He had not seen his friend this annoyed before. He was usual calm and collected. Then, Jenkins' mind wandered back to what Werner had tasked him with, and he pondered for a moment, wondering whether he should execute his instructions.

Werner's menacing warning crept into the front of his thoughts. Dire consequences if he failed to carry it out. He shuddered as if someone had opened a door allowing a draft that clawed at his warm skin. He sighed and walked over to his bag, pulled down the zip and brought out the bottle of water handed to him by Werner. His arm stretched out as he offered Fuller the bottle. His friend eyed the gift suspiciously. He did not recognise the brand.

"Take it. It's perfectly safe." Lied Jenkins, sensing his friend's trepidation. "It's a new brand that they're flogging at the club. It has an acquired taste but it's seemingly quite refreshing."

Fuller's hand reached out, paused for a moment as if he was trying to convince himself to take the offer, then his hand shot forward, snatching it from Jenkins. He twisted off the cap and guzzled down the cool liquid. With the bottle empty, he looked around for a bin, but Jenkins solved that problem by holding his hand out once more. "I'll dispose of it for you." He offered.

Fuller handed over the bottle and Jenkins stowed it away in his bag. Hiding the evidence. Fuller thanked him and the two continued with their game. It was not until the thirteenth hole that Fuller's complexion changed from the reddish weather-beaten colour to something closely resembling the pale white colour on Jenkins' bag.

His movement became stodgy as if he was suddenly walking through treacle. His speech laboured. Fuller stumbled but managed to remain upright. Jenkins looked across at his playing partner.

"Eric, are you alright?" He asked.

"I.... I...." Stuttered Fuller suddenly grabbing his left arm. He dropped to his knees. A look of impending doom on his face. A crushing weight pushing down on his chest. He was having a heart attack. He lifted an arm towards Jenkins in a vain attempt to ask silently for help but to his surprise, instead of stepping forward, his friend went in the opposite direction, out of arm's reach. "W... what the...." Fuller blurted out before collapsing to the ground.

The last thing he saw before losing consciousness was the darkened shape of Jenkins standing over him muttering something to himself. Fuller tried to speak but all that came out of his mouth was a sickening croak as his life left his body.

Jenkins stood there for a moment, hovering, before kneeling on one knee, placing his first two fingers at the side of Fuller's neck as he searched for a carotid pulse. Finding none, he reached into his jacket pocket and pulled out his mobile phone. He dialled one-one-two for the emergency operator.

"Emergency. What service please?" Asked the operator.

"Ambulance, please. There's been a terrible accident." Said Jenkins coldly.

2 – The Journey

The rain was tumbling out of the sky as if there was no tomorrow, coating everything in a watery film. Cars drove by, splashing in the puddles, which had formed in the small depressions in the road. Sometimes, splashing the water up onto the pavement, accidentally soaking any passers-by that were scurrying for cover. It had rained for most of the afternoon and into the early evening, depressing all who looked out on it.

Even the fading light of dusk could not hide the disappointment etched on people's faces, those that knew they had to head out into that. The streetlights tried their best to illuminate the gloom with varying degrees of success. Even the headlights of the cars struggled to pierce the curtain of water, which was now coming down in sheets, as if some unknown gigantic hand had turned on a tap fully.

He sat on his bed, the only two sources of light coming from a light on his bed side cabinet and from the tablet he was typing his report into. His wife had suggested earlier that he took a break from writing, but the truth had to be told. He knew he had an important meeting in the morning with some government types, yet unnamed, but he needed to save his evidence in a safe place as an insurance policy to protect himself and his family. He looked over at his bedside cabinet at the clock. Twenty-one forty.

Twelve hours from now, he would be on a bus travelling to the city to meet his contact. If all went well, he would return home that evening. If it went pear shaped, then at least the files he had stashed in a locker at the bus station before starting his journey, would have his back covered.

After tapping away on his tablet for another twenty minutes or so, he laid it down on the cabinet and slipped under the duvet. His head hit the soft pillows and almost immediately, fatigue overtook him, and he fell into a deep sleep. At least his body did. His mind, however, raced, trying to make sense of what he had done and was about to do.

The hours of research, hacking the main frame, being caught by the company's cyber security but disconnecting just in time. Did they know who he was? Where he stayed and the fact, he had a family? Was the risk worth it? People had to know what he had stumbled on to.

The authorities had to know. Had he done the right thing by contacting his old friend James Fuller? Had he put him in danger too? So many questions. His mind fought to make sense of them as his body tossed and turned. He was on his side one moment, on his back the next. Duvet on. Too hot. Duvet off. Too cold. Duvet back on and so the cycle continued.

The next thing he knew, his phone alarm was going off. He reached over and pulled it towards him, pressing the off button as he did so. He squinted, trying to focus his tired eyes on the phone screen. Zero-seven-thirty. He swore under his breath and kicked the duvet off. He lay there looking up at his bedroom ceiling.

A small spider scuttled its way across the whitewashed desert. He watched it effortlessly voyage across the ceiling avoiding the lampshade before disappearing behind the curtain rail.

Entertainment finished, he groaned and swung his legs over the side of the bed. His toes frantically searching for the safety and warmth of his slippers. They found one. Then the other. He shivered.

The normally toasty insides were freezing. He had forgotten to stick them under the radiator the night before, a ritual that he stuck to rigidly, except last night, obviously. He got up. The pain in his left shoulder was still there and it sent a piercing burst of pain to his brain to remind him. He winced.

Then reached over with his right hand, pressed his thumb on the area and did a couple of arm circles. Forward then back.

He continued until he heard something click. The pain had eased slightly. His movement was a little better, but he thought he would err on caution and go for a warm shower. He went downstairs cursing as he nearly tripped over a bag one of his daughters had left out, when she had stayed over last. He missed the two of them, but his wife had thought it better for them to go stay with her family until he had gotten his '*business*' sorted.

The house still smelled of them. The layers of different scents tickled his nostrils and the line of shoes under the radiator made him sigh a long-depressed sigh. He opened the bathroom door and went in. It was small but functional. A bath with an electric shower attached to the wall, a hand basin and, of course, a toilet.

He pulled back the shower curtain. Instantly, an electric shock of pain shot down his arm. He cursed again looking up at the light bulb in a vain attempt for relief. Reaching over to the controls, he pressed the button below the thermostat dial, which he had pre-set. A green light came on and a jet of warm water sprayed from the shower nozzle.

Wide spray or concentrated, he asked himself. Wide. He closed the curtain and stepped around it into the bath. The warm water hit his skin causing him to shiver momentarily before he got accustomed to the temperature.

He reached over and grabbed his shower gel, which was conveniently hanging on the small shelf under the shower, squeezed some of the dark blue liquid into his hand and then rubbed it onto his body lathering it up.

The smell was a pleasant 'clean' aroma. He washed his face with some of the excess gel before rinsing it off. He stood under the shower letting the warm water embrace him. His thoughts were silenced for a brief moment, and he just stood there enjoying the silence.

He returned to his bedroom to get dressed, picking a loose-fitting top and his favourite grey tracksuit bottom, with the maker's name in black writing, down the left leg from his hip down to just above his ankle. White sports socks and bright red trainers finished off the trendy ensemble. He looked at his watch as he picked it up and strapped it to his right wrist. A quarter to eight. Fifteen minutes!

His journey into nirvana had only lasted a quarter of an hour. The usual for him on an ordinary day but today was not ordinary. Not by a long shot. He had packed an overnight bag the previous night and he manhandled this downstairs.

Breakfast consisted of a mug of coffee, a splash of milk and half a tea spoonful of sugar. His wife had forgotten to get his favourite sugar substitute tablets.

A small bowl of cereal drowned in milk was wolfed down. Like the dutiful husband, he washed his dishes in a basin of soapy water, placed them on the drying rack next to the sink to dry, grabbing his jacket and overnight bag, and headed out the door, locking it. The sound of the lock clicking gave him a feeling of finality and this made him uneasy. The walk to the bus station took fifteen minutes.

During which he watched students from the university staggering about in various stages of intoxication. He had forgotten that this weekend was their annual 'let's piss off the locals' event, the official university name for it is 'Raisin Weekend' but it only lasted two days, normally the Saturday and Sunday of the second week in October.

The university is home to a large number of academic families – a tradition where older students adopt first year students as *'children'* and help guide them in a system of mentoring. This is, allegedly, a fantastic way for first year students to meet new people, and many of the friendships that begin as part of the academic family tradition continue throughout a student's time at the university and further.

However, in practice, it consists of the students getting absolutely smashed out of their faces on booze and causing havoc in the city centre and beyond.

There was a documented instance of one student buying a pre-packed sandwich at one famous supermarket chain, then heading a few hundred yards along the same street to ask for a refund on the same sandwich with a competing chain. On another occasion, half a dozen 'children' were reprimanded by two police officers for being in the historical and ornate fountain that inhabits the centre of Market Road.

They were told to get out or they would be reported to the university. A sad fact exists in this historic town that if said fountain incident had been perpetrated by a local, other than a student, then the locals would have been arrested. This student version would have been logged as a student prank by the police.

The man had once heard through his contacts, that a student had to be rescued by the lifeboat when they were overcome by hypothermia. They were in the sea wearing very little, intoxicated, and the temperature of the water was between five and fifteen degrees Celsius, in other words, bloody freezing!

This mentoring culminates in the aforementioned 'Raisin Weekend,' when 'children' are entertained by their 'parents' and are encouraged to play pranks and silly games. On Raisin Monday, the children dress in embarrassing costumes, are given strange objects with a traditional Latin inscription, and are let loose on lower college lawn for an enormous shaving foam fight. What the students and the university call tradition, even on their web pages, the locals dread it each year and it considered an embarrassment by most.

The man was disgusted by what he saw, so-called adults unable to stand, some of them, making their way in groups along the street cursing and swearing. Even in front of children.

What irked him the most was that, in years to come, these assholes would probably be either leading the country or at the head of some multi-million dollar company leading it into the abyss. He thanked his luck that he was going to be out of town for the culmination of the festivities. He stopped at a bakery and bought himself a sandwich and a bottle of water for the journey.

The bus station was quiet when he eventually got there. A couple of fellow travellers waited patiently in front of their modes of transport. There were three buses, each in its own bay. A couple had drivers already in them, but his bus was driverless. He joined the small queue of a couple of student types, each wearing large rucksacks on their backs.

Another three minutes went by before his driver arrived and went into the vehicle. He opened his little sanctum, where he was to sit for the next three hours, hung his jacket over the back of the seat, placed his money dispenser into it slot before pressing a button on the console in front of him, which activated the storage bays at the side of the bus.

They opened like giant mechanical bat wings. The two students deposited their sacks into the compartments that hissed shut before getting on. He took their money, as he settled into his chair, pressing a button at the side of the steering wheel, which allowed him to adjust it to a more comfortable position.

The man went into the station and up to the desk where a large woman sat behind a glass screen with slats cut in it to enable a conversation to be conducted. He asked how much it would cost for a locker and handed over the money. She pushed over his change and a key with a small circular tab attached on which was printed the number nine, ironically, his favourite number. He went over to the lockers and turned the key.

Unsurprisingly, it was empty. He looked through his overnight bag bringing out a large Manila envelope and put it into the locker before locking it. Then he went outside to join his fellow passengers.

The man paid his fare and took his place a couple of seats behind the driver. He had just sat down when the engine burst into life and with a lurch forward, his journey began. It had started to rain again making him glad of the shelter offered by the bus. He rummaged in his jacket pockets and found the book he had stashed there the night before. The book was entitled 'Fallon – Non Est

Optio Defectum.' The title translated from the Latin to mean 'Failure isn't an Option.'

It was the first in a series focusing upon a family linked to espionage. Opened it to the first page and began to read, immersing himself in the world of daring do. The book was new and had that new book smell. His wife had bought him it as one of a set of three for his birthday he had had recently.

It was by an unknown author who, foolishly, hoped that the monies from the book sales would help him retire from his current job but sadly, after forking out nine grand in loans, his return was a poultry ninety pounds, hardly what he had been expecting.

During the three-hour trip, he would occasionally look up from his book to see where they were. A woman, several rows behind him, entertained him with her loud telephone conversation, while a couple elsewhere, complained about the constant stops and starts. An old couple across the aisle from him, talked over their plans for the day, while devouring a large packet of crisps.

Each crunch was an assault on his senses. For once, the man wished he had brought his earphones, so that he could plug into his tablet, and drown out the ambient noise with some downloaded music he had saved on the device.

He moved in his seat. Stretching his left leg out into the isle, flexing, and relaxing the muscles, then he repeated the exercise, the best he could with the limited space, in his right leg. He managed a small back arch to try and loosen off his back. For the moment, his shoulder was staying quiet. The bus came to a stop at one of the many stations along his route. All the passengers got off including the woman having the telephone conversation, leaving just the man and the old couple.

The next stop, a large chested blonde got on, a woman with Down's syndrome, and a young boy. The bus was strangely quiet. The man looked briefly up from his book before returning to it.

The young boy decided to put his music on, annoying the blonde. He apologised, putting his volume down, before pushing in his earphones. He smiled at the blonde, like an army general whose forces had just won a victory. The man was oblivious to this as he was lost in the tales of daring do in his book.

A sign for boarding kennels flashed by on his left as cars and lorries zoomed by on the right. The clouds were now heavy with rain. So heavy that visibility was poor outside. Every so often, a motorway sign would flash up in bright orange writing a warning about surface water as lines of cars and vans crawled their way forwards.

After three hours, the bus pulled lazily into the station. The man got off the vehicle after thanking the driver. His body was complaining of the long period of inactivity. Knees, back, and legs had joined his shoulder to make an orchestral movement to pain. He searched his bag for some relief and found a box of painkillers.

Pressed two tablets out of their foil wrapper and popped them into his mouth. Swallowing them dry, which he hated doing. He went into the main concourse of the station and looked up at the timetable. Ten minutes till his connection. He checked his watch before double checking the board. Better to be safe than sorry, he thought. Stance nine.

He made his way around to stance nine and stood with several other passengers. The bus was in. An impressive looking vehicle. The bottom deck consisted of the driver's cabin and storage, whilst the top deck was seating and at the rear, toilets. It looked like an escapee from a science fiction movie rather than a mode of transport. The man wondered if it had a transporter device in the rear.

Pigeons dodged under foot. Cooing and flapping their wings as each fought for scraps. One with mottled plumage, black and white speckles, stood out reminding the man of a pepper pot with wings. Even the driver, a tall bald-headed man, commented on it as he opened the vehicle access door.

After a few minutes checking the vehicle over, the driver signalled for people to board. A passenger climbed on and used the local term for his destination but had to repeat himself, using the proper name, when the driver looked back at him blankly.

The man smiled. After a five-minute wait, the engine burst into life and the second half of the man's journey had begun. This time it would be shorter – forty minutes, the timetable assured him. The scenery would be different too. What had been open fields filled with cows and sheep gave way to high rise tenements and built-up areas.

He plugged his tablet into an available charging point, sitting back in the luxurious leather chair, plugging in his headphones, the same headphones he was wishing he had brought earlier, he had found in a small little used pocket on his jacket. He scrolled through his music playlists before picking some movie themes.

Pressed play and closed his eyes. Lost in a mixture of his thoughts and the music being piped through his headphones, the second half of the journey was over as quickly as it had begun as the man was woken from his catnap by the jolt of the bus stopping.

He gathered both his stuff and his thoughts before getting off. The terminus for the space age bus was a small station. He looked around and soon spotted the taxi rank filled with several types and colours of cars. Taxi rank etiquette dictated that he went to the car at the head of the rank. It was a battered BMW that had seen better days.

The stench of air freshener did little to mask the perfume of cooked food and vomit that assaulted his nostrils as he got in the back. The driver, a male in his mid-fifties with tattoo covered arms and earrings in both lobes, turned round, and welcomed him.

"Where to, mate?"

"The New Mill Hotel, please." Said the man.

'No worries." Said the driver pushing down his meter, starting its count.

The man pulled out his book again and tried to distract himself by reading a few more pages. The nerves were beginning to kick in. His stomach was hosting a trampolining championship for butterflies or at least, that's what it felt like. He was bounced about quite a bit in the back of the taxi as the driver made it his mission to hit every single pothole, going back for seconds.

The man's shoulder had woken up from its slumber, and in the confined space of the back of the taxi, he tried his best to first do neck circles with little success, moving to an arm circle or two. He noticed the taxi driver's eyes darting from the road to his mirror and back, watching him. The man stopped his therapy and sat motionless for the rest of the journey to the hotel.

3 – New Mill Hotel

The New Mill Hotel was a good hour away from the bus terminus. Six storeys of a converted mill, it is listed as a world heritage site, and has several touristy things happening on the site, some linked to the stay at the hotel. He paid the taxi and went through the glass doored entrance into a spacious reception area.

Round to his right was a lift, he presumed to the other floors, the reception desk was 'manned' by a young woman, in her late twenties, with brown hair tied in a ponytail, dressed all in black. Her gold name badge said her name was Kirsten. She looked up and smiled as the man approached the desk.

"Good afternoon, sir." She said from behind a glass screen. The man could about hear her. "Welcome to the New Mill Hotel. How can I help you today?"

"I'd like to check in please."

"I'm afraid check-in isn't until three o'clock, as housekeeping are still readying the rooms. If you'd like to either take a seat either here or in the bar, someone will call you when your room is ready." The man nodded and looked around for a seat.

There were several options – three sets of two couches facing each other, with a white painted table in the middle, and two high backed leather chairs made up each rest area. A metal staircase spiralled its way up to the second floor which, going by the smell coming from there, led to the restaurant.

A piano sat begging to be played under the stairs. To his left was a corridor leading to the bar area and according to the sign on the wall, led on from the bar to the leisure facilities (swimming pool and spa). Against the wall as you walked towards the bar were doors to the toilets, men's then females. On the wall hung various pictures of the site through the centuries.

The man took little interest in these, as he sat down on one of the upholstered couches but not before rearranging the cushions, three per couch. He took out his book and started to read where he left off. Again, as before, he was starting to get engrossed in the fictitious spy's adventures when Kirsten made the announcement from behind the desk, saying the rooms were ready.

The man stashed his book and got to his feet, filled in the required documents, and was handed his welcome pack, which contained leaflets about various activities happening in and around the building, a brief history of it, and his room key.

"Would you like to book dinner tonight?"

"Seven thirty would be fine." Suggested the man. Kirsten scanned through the pages on the computer screen.

"Seven thirty?" She repeated to confirm. The man nodded. "That's you booked in. Is there anything else I can help you with, sir?"

"Yes, there is." The man began putting his hand in his jacket breast pocket and bringing out a small envelope. "Can you keep this in a safe place for me? A friend will be coming to collect it if I'm not here. A Mr. Whitestone." Kirsten took a pen from her jacket pocket and scribbled the name down repeating it back to him, taking delivery of the envelope, scribbling "FOA Mr. Whitestone."

"I'll put it in the safe for you, sir, and I'll leave a note in the diary on the computer."

"Thank you."

"No problem." She disappeared for a moment to deposit the envelope in the safe before coming back and typing something on the screen.

He climbed into the lift and pressed for the sixth floor because, according to the sign, stuck to the side of the button panel, which was the floor his room was. First were staff quarters, second reception, third the restaurant, fourth were the function rooms named after the founder of the old mill, and the last two were the bedroom floors.

The lift lurched into movement, momentarily leaving his stomach behind, as lifts tend to do, and went up to the sixth floor. He followed the arrows on the walls, through a couple of heavy fire doors, and found his room. Inserting his electronic key card, the light flickered green, and the door unlocked. He pushed the door open and went in, closing the door behind him.

The room was spacious with two large windows spoiling him with the amount of natural light they were letting in. Immediately to the left of the entrance were your storage areas, two wardrobes complete with four hangars in each. To your right was the bathroom with a toilet, wash basin, bath, and shower, connected to the wall. Four towels hung neatly folded on the heated towel rail behind the door.

The double bed was huge, to the extent that he thought he might need a map to traverse from one side to the other, four pillows were stacked in pairs beside each other, and a piece of cloth was draped around the duvet, its purpose escaped him, a dressing table looked across at him from the bed, over which hung a heavy looking mirror.

The dressing table had a couple of drawers on the left and a pull-out shelf, where some kind person had put out a tray, with a kettle on it, a couple of white mugs and a choice of coffee sachets, tea, and a few hot chocolates. A television was positioned to the far right, just at the right level to watch from the bed, its remote-control sitting waiting in front of the device.

He threw his bag on the bed, took off his jacket and hung it up in the wardrobe, taking a few minutes to figure out how to unhook the hangar. He retrieved the remote control for the television and pressed the 'on' button. Nothing happened. He pressed again. Nothing.

Damn it! He had forgotten to switch the power on at the wall. He felt a right proper fool. Eureka! The tv burst into life. Some documentary was on about the mating habits of big horned sheep. He kicked his shoes off and dived headfirst on to the bed.

Next thing he knew, his alarm on his phone was going off. It was nineteen hundred hours. He got up and went through to the bathroom and switched on the shower. It was more powerful than the one at home, and harder to use than his own. After a few moments fiddling with knobs, the water flowed and the shower gel, made of sea kelp, if you believed the label, smelt great and made him feel the same. Casual clothes were the order of the evening.

A loose-fitting shirt, dark coloured cargo pants and trainers. He went out into the corridor, along to the lift, and pressed the call button. After what seemed like ages, the doors hissed open. It was empty. He got in. The doors hissed closed, pressed three and the lift started to move.

The doors hissed open once more revealing the expanse that was the restaurant. To the man's right was the welcome desk, complete with electronic till. A stout woman dressed in a smart black skirt and flowery blouse approached. She smiled warmly.

"Table for one?" She asked in a broad local accent, then escorted him to a table. A napkin was folded on it, containing his cutlery (fork, spoon, and knife). A glass and ribbed tumbler stood like soldiers on guard. She pulled the chair out slightly inviting him to sit. "Do you want anything to drink?"

"A bottle of the house wine, please."

"White or red?"

"White."

"Thank you. I'll bring you some complimentary water as well." The woman left returning with both the wine and the water, ably assisted by one of the other waiting staff. The wine, a Pinot Grigio La Casada Italy, was crisp, cold and a little fruity as it hit the back of his throat. It was only a sip. A taster if you like as the bottle taunted him from the ice cooler on the table. His meal was lovely and filling.

His starter was a cheesy quiche, dressed rocket salad leaves, a drizzle of balsamic vinegar, and sun-dried tomatoes. His main was beer and steak pie, buttered mash potatoes, with a side of green beans, and sliced carrot. The dessert was a vanilla panna cotta, sliced strawberries, strawberry sauce, macaroon, and a pink champagne ice cream. Delicious.

Washed down by his Pinot. Full and satisfied, the man took the rest of his bottle downstairs, and found a vacant couch, where he sat savouring his drink and watched people. He found it far more entertaining than his book or working on his tablet.

A group of tourists caught his attention, due to the volume of their voices. They wanted the whole hotel to know their business. One of the men sporadically sounded as though he was trying to cough his guts up, whilst his wife moaned about the speed of service at dinner.

The man wanted to comment but refrained. Instead, he just sat there absorbing their self-righteousness adding the odd shake of his head, when he disagreed with anything they said, as he masked his covert listening by pretending to look through a newspaper, he had picked up from the table.

A woman approached reception and was greeted by Kirsten's welcoming smile. She asked how she could help, and that was an invitation to open the flood gates of complaints.

"The room isn't laid out the way I requested." Began the woman.

"Okay. What room number are you?" Asked Kirsten taking a deep breath. The man's interest was piqued.

"Fourteen."

"What seems to be the trouble?"

"I specifically asked for single beds, and I have been given a double."

"Ah. Did you ask for two singles when you booked?"

"I always get this when I stay here!" Exclaimed the woman, the volume of her voice starting to rise. Kirsten, give her credit where credit is due, stayed calm and collected.

"I don't see it in your notes." Relayed Kirsten.

"I booked over the phone..."

"But did you request the singles?"

"You should know who I am when I book. I am a regular customer here."

"I'm sorry madam, but unless you state at the time of booking, there isn't thing I can do." Apologised Kirsten.

"What? Nothing! Can't you move me to another room?"

"Sorry. I can't move you as we are fully booked."

2 8

"Well, this is disgraceful! I've never been treated like this; in all the times I've been coming here!" Exclaimed the woman becoming quite agitated. The man watched on with interest. Kirsten picked up the telephone, had a brief conversation and put it down again.

"The manager is on his way, and he'll discuss the situation with you." Said Kirsten, clearly glad that the glass screen was there, forming a barrier between them.

The incident seemed to cool suddenly until a tall dark-haired man in a smart dark suit appeared from the lift. He walked past the woman and went behind into reception, him and Kirsten disappeared into the small room at the back of reception, only to appear moments later, the man in the suit taking charge.

The man was bored, yawned, first looking at his watch, 2200, and then at his empty glass now mirrored by the empty bottle. Time for bed. He said goodnight to Kirsten, who smiled, and took the lift to the sixth. He had closed the curtains on both windows earlier but left one of the windows open allowing the noise of the rushing water, of the river below, to filter into his room.

He thought the sound of rushing water would act as a calming influence on his feverish brain. Entering the room, he put his key card into the holder on the wall, reversing the card, and this activated the electrics. He tossed off his clothes on to the floor and switched the lights out.

He quickly regretted this decision, as he hit his knee on the edge of the bed, making him curse aloud. He slowly felt his way around the bed before climbing in. It was not long before he was tucked up in bed and he slowly started to drift off. But the people in the room next door had other ideas, as they cranked up the volume of their television to such a level, that the man could hear every syllable of what the person on screen was saying.

The man groaned and turned over pulling the pillow around his head like giant earmuffs. It did not help. He turned over to the other side. Finally, he got up and juggled with the ideas of either banging on the wall, their room door and confronting the assholes, or phoning down to reception, and letting them deal with it.

He chose reception, picked up the handset of the telephone next to his bed, dialled zero and waited. The phone buzzed three times before Kirsten's voice came on.

"Reception. Kirsten speaking." The man explained the situation and said that he did not mind people watching television in their rooms, but it was past eleven and the volume was extremely loud. Kirsten apologised, saying, she would do something about it.

The man thanked her and put the receiver down. He lay there on his back and waited. Television blaring. He looked at his watch. Twenty-three twenty. Television still blaring and so it went on until midnight. He wondered whether he should call reception again or go down in person.

The latter was his choice this time. He got dressed in his joggers, loose top and did not bother tying his laces. Opened the door and went out into the corridor.

Walked past his neighbours and to his utter disbelief, the television seemed to have gotten louder. That made his mind up. He walked round the corner to be greeted by the woman from the restaurant, and a male member of staff sitting on a couch opposite one of the lifts.

She asked if everything was okay, and the man explained the situation. She said she would deal with it. The man also said he had contacted reception, and nothing had been done. The woman apologised and got up, saying she would find the underlying cause of it.

Satisfied, the man returned to his room and his bed. The television was blaring. Then the sound of a phone ringing added to the cacophony. Television blaring. Telephone ringing. Then nothing. A knock came. Was that on his door?

The man was not sure. He waited. Ears straining. The knock came again. It was his door. He got up and put on his joggers. Unlocked the door and popped his head around to see the same man that had sitting with the woman from the restaurant.

"Problem dealt with, sir. The couple had fallen asleep and didn't even answer our telephone calls. We had to come up and knock on the door." Informed the man called 'Steve.' The man thanked him and closed the door. It turns out the couple in the room next to the man were partially deaf too.

Room service would later show them how to access the subtitle facility on the television. He returned to bed and fell asleep. A restless one but he did sleep until his alarm went off at eight o'clock.

Eventually, the man emerged from his room, dark circles under his eyes. The cocktail of the assholes next door, and the super soft pillows, made his sleep, one from hell. He weaved his way along the corridors to the lift, pressing the call button. The doors hissed open instantly which caught him by surprise. He got in and pressed three for the restaurant.

It lurched and then moved. The number above the floor buttons counting down in red. It reached three. The doors hissed open, and the man exited. The restaurant was terribly busy.

The same woman that had greeted him the previous night repeated the procedure and showed him to a table at the opposite end of the floor. He ordered his coffee and then his breakfast.

Fresh yoghurt with muesli on top followed by a full Scottish breakfast which, for those not sure, consists of bacon, square sausage, normal sausage, mushrooms, a sliced tomato, a dollop of baked beans, black pudding, potato scone, haggis, and a choice of the way your egg was prepared, in the man's case, scrambled.

Plus, two slices of slightly burnt toast accompanied on a small side plate by two piece of butter and a portion of marmalade and strawberry jam. All washed down by the strongest coffee the man had ever drank. The whole meal took just over an hour to devour, as he enjoyed another round of his favourite game show – people watching.

He recognised several people from the night before. The couple arguing about the speed and quality of service. An older couple, two tables over, talking with the volume control switched to high. They moved to the top of his suspect list for the inhabitants of the room next to him. He instantly started throwing them visual daggers, subtly though. So subtle, they did not notice, but it made the man feel a lot better.

His attention was drawn to a couple off to the left. The woman had her back to him, but the man was facing him and reminded him of the mad professor from the 'Back to the Future' movies. They were in deep conversation about the meal they were eating, analysing every mouthful. The man shook his head in disbelief.

A group of about seven, over to the back of the restaurant, were loudly discussing the schedule for the day. It turns out, the bulk of the people at this scene, were on a two-day bus tour of the area.

One of the older men coughed sporadically making the man cringe as he felt every painful exhale. After each cough, the gentleman would look around for either sympathy or to see if anyone had noticed his discomfort – he received neither.

The man finished his meal with one more mouthful of coffee before heading downstairs and then up to his room via the lift. He grabbed his jacket and went back down to reception and through the exit.

A large touring bus was parked over the other side of the car park. It had a huge red rose emblazoned on the side of it, as well as the name of the county the bus was from. The type of customers up in the restaurant now made sense to the man. He zipped up his jacket and pulled the collar up to protect his neck as it began to rain again.

The deluge this time was what the locals call drizzle – the super fine droplets that cling to everything like a wet carpet.

For a split second, he wondered whether his walk would be enjoyable in this weather but after a brief discussion with himself, he decided to plod on.

He walked past a huge building on his right that matched the hotel in stature. This housed a museum dedicated to times long gone in the weaving industry, a sandwich board posted outside an open door, promising a café at the end of your journey.

The picture of a badger on the wall enticed you to follow him to the Clyde Valley waterfall. The man took up the invitation and started to climb up some wooden steps. These took him to the beginning of a wooded area.

Some thoughtful people had added a carpet of wire mesh on the path to aid with traction. He went up and round, stopping to read the occasional sign that kept you informed of the local flora and fauna. At the top of the hill, he came to a fork in the path.

The left fork continued the climb whilst the right one took you down to an observation platform closer to the river. He chose the right-hand path. The observation platform opened through the low-lying foliage allowing you to see and hear the power of the river.

The water was tumbling down over a mini waterfall, the colour of the underlying rocks melding with the water causing a pale stripy effect. He stood there for a while taking in the sheer majesty of the vista before backtracking and continuing his climb.

At the top of the next rise, he came across several large pipes coming down the hill. A sign nearby let passers-by know that these pipes fed the local power station which was just around the next bend. A large turbine was cemented into the ground and a small passage on the sign referenced it.

The man continued, walking past the aforementioned power station which, by his standards, was a disappointing square building surrounded by a high fence.

Next treasure on his hunt was a large mural on a storage building of a badger. Very impressive but spoiled by some ned's graffiti to the left of it. A two-storey house was next as he trudged through muddy puddles, and the path was becoming increasingly treacherous. Steadying himself a few times as his feet lost traction.

A pile of logs was neatly stacked at the side of the building. There were posters advertising various demonstration rallies plastered in the windows, leaving just enough space to allow light in. Two cars were parked at the end of the house, a family hatchback, and a land rover.

Both looked as if they had been there for a while, going by the length of grass that had grown up underneath them. He looked up ahead, more dirt track that was slowly turning muddy, weighed up his options and decided to turn back, retracing his steps.

Unknown to the man, his journey was being seen, the same black BMW that had dropped him off, had appeared at the top of the track, just as he had turned to head back. The driver door opened, and the tattooed man got out, reached in, and grabbed his jacket before locking the door.

He waited until the man was sufficiently ahead of him before following at a discrete distance. Just keeping back enough not to arouse suspicion. He put his hands in his pockets and quickened his pace a little.

The man ahead was oblivious to his pursuer. He ambled along as if he didn't have a care in the world. When he got to the top of the rise, he noticed another path that took him further into the woods and, after a quick time check, he decided to go on this little adventure. He popped his earphones in and pressed play on the music app on his phone.

A theme from one of his favourite war movies came on as he took the new path.

Fallen leaves obscured the path and sometimes made it difficult to follow so he had to concentrate a lot more than on the outward journey. His concentration blocked his awareness of being followed. Tattooed man was still there and had taken the same path.

It twisted and turned for about half a mile before coming out at another observation platform. This time above some cliffs. Spectacular rock formations, striped horizontally, making it look like some kind of layered cake one might get at a bakery.

A small shrine had been erected commemorating someone who had jumped, thought the man, as he looked down at the cards, a stuffed teddy bear, and a bouquet of flowers that had seen better days.

The man's heart suddenly felt heavy with sadness. He read one of the cards and going by what was written, the man surmised that the shrine was for a teenager that had taken her own life. He bowed his head in silent respect before realising he was not alone. He pulled his earphones out as he turned to see the tattooed man standing there. A look of shock appeared on his face. His hands raised up in a defensive pose.

"What are you doing here?" He asked.

"The boss wants what you've taken." Demanded the tattooed man pulling out a silenced automatic, aiming it at the man.

"I don't know what you're talking about."

"We know what you've taken, and we want it back."

"I don't have it anymore."

"Wrong answer." The automatic spat twice, making the man grab his chest, dropping first to his knees, then falling face down in the leaf litter. Tattooed man put his weapon away and stepped forward giving the man's body a swift kick to make sure he was dead.

No movement. He crouched down, and searched the body, retrieving the man's phone, putting it in his pocket. He found the man's wallet, opened it, took the money, and the cards, before tossing it.

He then picked up the corpse and after a little struggle, threw it over the barrier. It turned a couple of times before hitting the water with a splash, resurfacing with him face down, the current took hold, pulling him down river. The corpse looked like how someone would look if they were going down a water slide at one of those aqua parks.

4 – Bad News

The phone chirped on the bedside table, and an arm snaked out from under the duvet, fumbled for a minute looking for it, got it, pulling it back under, like a spider taking its freshly caught prey back into its lair. There was a muffled conversation and then the covers were thrown back revealing a man in his mid-forties with a well-defined physique and wearing boxer shorts.

"I'm sorry Mr. Fuller, your father passed away last week."

"What do you mean he's dead? He called me last week." The man sat up. A look of disbelief on his face. He scratched his head, as if he were trying to shake his brain into overdrive to try and understand the news. "How did he die?"

"Heart attack. There has been an autopsy."

"Heart attack? How? The guy was super fit for his age."

"I'm sorry sir, but I don't have access to that information. We were wondering whether you could come to his house and sort out his affairs?"

"Yeah, sure." Fuller switched off the phone lying back on his bed, staring up at the ceiling. He did not cry. There was no emotion. Yes, he had spoken to his father last week on the phone, but they did not really get on or have that kind of relationship.

The shrinks at the clinic called it '*an estranged relationship.*' The only thing Fuller knew for sure was that his father was researching an incident that happened during the Second World War, but he was not sure whether his father was involved or not.

It took him an hour to shower, shave and get dressed. He weighed up his options – take the car or jump on the bus. Public transport won. He hooked the elastic hoops of his face mask over his ears as he stepped onto the bus. He mumbled his destination to the driver and paid the fare before finding a vacant seat which, at this present time, was easy as the bus was almost empty.

He idled the time away by skimming through a magazine one of the other passengers had left on the seat. His eyes fell upon a short story, no more than eight hundred words by someone called Robyn Smythe. It was called 'Condensation on a Window.' He started to read.

'The rain is coming down in sheets on the other side of the condensation covered window. I sit on my bed, my concentration switching between typing this and watching the television program playing off to my left. My body hurts. My mind is a swirl of thoughts and emotions.

The first day of the new year dawned almost twelve hours ago and all I have done is had breakfast consisting of an americano coffee and cereal. I hate this time of year, the build up from the beginning of December, presents getting bought, adverts, on the television promising excitement on the hallowed box that is the centre of every living room.

Those same presents get wrapped with decorative paper only for you to realise that you are crap at wrapping, and you have not got enough to fulfil the task. You curse, throw the scissors across the bed and watch them bounce like a toddler's attempt at a javelin throw at the kindergarten Olympics until they come to rest precariously teetering on the edge of the bed.

A conversation with your oldest child that goes pair shaped because she is offended by your tone of voice only blossoms into an all-out verbal slagging match with your wife when your daughter toddles off and grasses you up to her.

The place of the dressing down was in the middle of the street and your daughter found that highly inappropriate. Sitting on the toilet with your trousers around your ankles, now that is what I call inappropriate.

I have noticed, since the pandemic, that people are more easily offended or is that just me? I mean, I have been on this planet of ours for almost six decades and I have never known it so difficult to voice an opinion without annoying someone or some group.

Even the classic comedy series I grew up with, now have disclaimers at the start warning people of content that they may find offensive.

Hogmanay, or New Year's Eve, is celebrated for me as it always is, sitting downstairs alone with the rest of the family upstairs tucked up snuggly in bed. The sound of cars slowly diminishes as we approach the bells.

I glance at the clock on the windowsill to realise it is obscured by a couple of cheesy Christmas cards. I ponder for a moment whether it is worth the effort to get up and move the obstruction or to take the lazier choice and press the remote-control button.

The latter wins. Two minutes to go. I press play on my program and take a sip of my beverage of choice, Irish whisky crème on the rocks. The alcohol hits the back of my throat, the mixture of the warmth from the alcohol and the shock of the cold from the ice sums up how I feel at that precise moment. Sadness over the end of a terrible year of decisions and disappointments mixed with anticipation of what the new year holds. Maybe another two books published under my pseudonym.

My youngest daughter leaving the cotton wool confines of secondary school and branching out either into the next stage of academia or a part-time post at my place of work. My oldest hits twenty-one squarely in the face and this takes her to the three-quarter mark of her university degree.

The prospect of a caravanning holiday to celebrate her milestone in life fills me full of dread. We will return to one of the sites that holds significance to our family but also the one where you need mountaineering training to ascend the hills the site is perched on. Hence, my lack of enthusiasm.

A car goes past the house. The condensation is still hanging on to the inside of the window like my hopes for the coming year. Riverettes of water trickle down the pane like tiny tsunamis of time passing by. The radiator must be on.

My Yoda water bottle, propped up against the window, looking out on the world, moves slightly, catches me momentarily off guard. I regain my composure, and my gaze is transfixed by a piece of grass that is hanging from the guttering directly outside the window. It is moving up and down in the wind like a conductor's baton as it conducts some silent rainy symphony.

I have three hundred and sixty-four days to see what happens. I am considering scaling back on my workload, a decision that my not please some people at my place of employment. I mean, I have done my time, my body is complaining. My back hurts.

My knees are creaking like old timber floorboards. I have had enough. I sit here, my iPad sitting on bent knees, typing this, waiting to see what this brand spanking new year is going to throw at me.'

The piece made him feel uplifted. Knowing that someone else's life was worse than his. The journey that he had embarked on had been weighing heavily on his mind.

The information he had stumbled upon during his research was like a millstone around his neck. A burden that he would be glad to get rid of when he met his contact.

After twenty minutes, the bus pulled up to his stop, he left the magazine where he had found it and made his way down the aisle towards the front of the bus, nodded his thanks to the driver and got off. Walked another few minutes before stopping outside a semi-detached house with a white door.

He climbed a couple of steps and paused at the door. Took a deep breath before putting the key in the lock and going in. The house was an upstairs / downstairs with three bedrooms upstairs and a dining room, kitchen, and bathroom downstairs.

The hallway was in darkness and the whole place had a musky old person smell about it. He put on the light next to the telephone, which was next to the door. The damn energy saving bulb, only lit up the small alcove the table was in and very little else! He went into the dining room and was shocked by what he saw – chaos.

There were stacks of paper everywhere – on the floor, on the dining room table and even on top of the television. There was a desk in front of the window, in front of which was a large leather backed chair.

On the desk was a notepad, several pencils of various grades, a desk lamp and a transparent plastic desk organiser that had six receptacles – one, a tall cylinder shape, had two rulers; a pair of black handled scissors and a roll of Sellotape hooked over the rulers. Another, a smaller cylinder, had several more pencils in it.

One had what looked like small metal screwdrivers, another had a sharpener while the last two contained a couple of thumb drives for a computer and an adapter for downloading pictures from a digital camera memory card.

He switched on the desk lamp and flicked open the notepad. It was then that he realised he was not alone. Something being forced into the small of his back also helped. He instinctively raised his hands.

"Please. Do not do anything stupid." Said a heavily accented man's voice. Fuller could not place the accent. "Why are you here?"

"This is my father's house and I'm going through his belongings."

"Have you found it yet?"

"Found what?"

"Don't play with me!" Yelled the man and punched Fuller in the left kidney, forcing him to crumple down to his left knee. "Get up!" Fuller slowly got to his feet. "Where is it?"

"I have no idea what you're talking about." Fuller began to turn slowly and then the lights went out as the butt of the pistol connected with the back of his head.

5 – A Secret Past

A few hours later, Fuller regained his senses and found himself lying on his back looking up at the ceiling. Both his jacket and trouser pockets were turned inside out as if they had been searched. The thumping sore head he now had, reminded him of what had happened.

He slowly got to his feet and surveyed the room in front of him. Tossed. Stacks of files knocked over on to the floor, drawers open, and the top of his father's desk, items scattered. He staggered over to the desk and looked at the desk organiser, the drives were gone.

"Damn it!" He cursed thumping the desk top hard with his fist. He looked around the rest of the house, but nothing looked out of place, so he turned out the lights, locked the front door and went out into the street.

He stopped at the bottom of the stairs and manipulated his head by moving it from side to side, backwards and forwards. Yip, it was still connected to his neck. He placed his hand on the area that was throbbing and found a huge lump.

'Need to put some ice on that when I get home and then I have a grudge to settle.' He thought as he moved off to the nearest bus top, still swaying slightly.

An elderly woman glared at him disapprovingly. He smiled, raised a hand to signal he was all right, but kept walking still sensing the look from the woman. The flat door swung open, and he almost fell through the doorway. He cursed as he checked the back of his head again.

The lump was now the size of a tennis ball. He kicked the door shut with his heel and went into the kitchen, rummaged in the freezer, pulled out a frozen bag of peas, and placed it gingerly on the back of his neck. The couch was screaming his name, so he obliged and crumpled into it like a tree being felled. He lay there looking up at the ceiling going over the last few hours in his head.

'Dad's dead. He dies suddenly but this does not make sense as he was extremely fit for his age. Hell, he liked his golf, did daily swims at the local swimming pool, had a gym membership. It just does not make sense. I get the phone call and turn up at his house, a place I have not been to in at least a decade, only to find some asshole with a gun already there and looking for something that belonged to Dad.

I get this melon on my head for my troubles, and the place gets tossed. Was the asshole already there going through Dad's stuff and I interrupted him, or did he follow me? Did our friend with the gun find what he was looking for or did he leave empty handed? I'll need to go back to the house in the morning and have another look.'

With his mind made up, he succumbed to the blow again and fell asleep.

He was awakened by a banging on his front door. He got up and noticed that the peas were no longer frozen and there was a wet patch on the pillow where moments earlier, his head had been resting. He turned the handle and opened the door. It was the postman.

"Alright squire." The postman chirped like some irritating bird. Fuller grunted. "Got a packet for a Mister Gregor Fuller. Is that you mate?"

Another grunt.

The postman handed over a small-padded envelope. Then thrust a small clipboard towards him. "Gotta sign for it mate." Handing him a standard cheap looking biro pen. Fuller scribbled his signature and closed the door.

'*Who was the hell sending him a package?*' He thought as he examined it. Sure, it had his name on it and the address was the right one but there was no return address. He moved it up and down as if on an imaginary set of scales.

Seemed light. Walked over to the main window, and took out his pocketknife, he always carried in his left trouser pocket, flicked open the blade and slid it under the flap of the envelope and slowly and carefully drew the blade away from himself thus opening the packet. He pushed the sides together opening the throat of the packet a little allowing him to investigate it.

There was a piece of paper and a red thumb drive. He tipped the contents onto the table by the window and stood motionless staring at it for a moment. He picked up the letter. It was a standard piece of note paper. The same type that was on his father's desk. A note had been scribbled on to it.

'*Gregor. If you are reading this, then the bastards have caught up with me. Don't believe my death as natural causes because it wasn't. I've been researching an old mission that has just been declassified, that I took part in in the war, and I've found some discrepancies between the official version and the copy I have (on the thumb drive).*'

'*I tried to keep you away from the business, but I've failed and for that, son, I am truly sorry.*' His father apologising. 'Never. He wasn't that type of man. He continued, '*I never told you how proud I was when you joined the Army, but I was.*

I know you thought I was angry with you, when you opted out of university before the end of your course, but when you joined the Special Forces unit (I still had my old contacts), I was beaming with pride. Please take my findings to my old friend at Intelligence House in the capital, colonel James Scott. He'll know what to do. DO NOT open the drive or get involved.

DAD x'

Fuller wiped a tear from his eye. "What the hell have you gotten yourself into Dad?" He walked over to where his laptop was sitting and switched it on. It blinked, whirred, and then up popped his screensaver – a picture of a snow-capped mountain.

Then a box came up asking for his password. He typed it in, waited until the screen had settled down, before placing the thumb drive in the side of the device in one of the two available ports and instantly, the contents of the drive popped up on screen.

There were several files. '*Operation Hummingbird.*' '*Das Wolfsrudel.*' '*The Office of Special Projects*' and '*Operation Dionysus.*' Fuller went back to his dad's old house, a little warier than he was the first time. This time, however, the front door was locked, and he had to use his key to get in. He pushed the door open slowly but there was something on the floor blocking it opening properly.

Fuller popped his head round and looked down. Another envelope was lying there. He eventually got in and picked up the second envelope.

It was addressed to his father. He opened it and found a thick file with a note attached.

'*Dear James, if you are reading this, then I am either in grave danger or dead. The file I have enclosed is to be kept by you as insurance. If anything happens to me, you must deliver it to colonel James Scott at the Office of Special Projects in London. I cannot stress the urgency of my request. I hope I find you well.*

Robert Foster.'

First, the cryptic message from beyond the grave and now this. What had his father been up to? It certainly was not a quiet retirement. Fuller's head was spinning.

6 – Dexter

Several hours before this, in an office somewhere in London, James Scott sat at his desk skimming through the pages of a file. His furrowed brow and the odd sharp intake of breath conveyed the seriousness of what he was digesting. A knock came on his office door.

"Enter."

The door opened and in walked one of his operatives, Fiona '*Dex*' Dexter. She was of average height; olive skin and short dark hair cut in a bob. She closed the door and almost glided across the floor to stand poker straight at attention in front of her section chief.

"Relax Dexter. Take a seat."

He closed the file and looked over at the young woman.

"What do you know about '*Operation Dionysus*?'"

"A top-secret operation during the Second World War, mounted by the Allies, to stop the Germans from producing some kind of super drug, which would allow their forces to basically keep going without the need of sleep or food, or something like that."

Scott smiled a fatherly smile, impressed at his young operative's knowledge. "But that happened seventy-eight years ago sir. It's old news. Why the sudden interest now?"

"Because what is written in the history books, Dexter, isn't the whole story." He handed her the file he had been reading when she had arrived. "The truth has been twisted a little by the passage of time. Almost shattered if you like." Dexter looked at the folder and took in the name embossed across the front of it in big black capital letters. '*Operation Shattered Truth*.'

Scott watched as the colour drained from Dexter's face. "There has been some renewed interest in the wartime operation by one of our former operatives. Sadly, his investigations didn't end well." Dexter swallowed hard, "I want you to take a look at this and do some damage limitation."

"But sir," protested Dexter, "this is a job for an experience field agent. I'm just an analyst with only four years' experience…"

Scott raised a hand and stopped her in mid-sentence.

"And you want to know why I picked you? Someone with, as you have quite rightly said, limited experience and you don't have your 'K' number yet…"

Dexter nodded.

"Two reasons. Firstly, according to your file, you are a bit of a history enthusiast with a good knowledge for facts and figures."

He paused and looked across at her. She looked overwhelmed by what he had just said. "Secondly and more importantly, my superiors want this handled delicately and not, as one of the field agents might do, handle it like a bull in a China shop." Dexter nodded and got up to leave. "Dexter."

"Sir?"

"Stop this at all costs. No matter what." She nodded. "And you do have your firearm proficiency training?" Again, Dexter nodded. "Good. Go to the armoury and pick up your sidearm."

Dexter opened the door and closed it behind her. She stood there for a moment, trying to both gather her thoughts and regulate her breathing. She was almost hyper-ventilating, or it felt like that. The old woman that sat behind the desk outside Scott's office looked across at her. Dexter smiled a nervous smile and left. She went down the corridor to the lift and pressed the button to summon it.

While she waited, she opened the file and started to speed read the contents, trying to commit the information and pictures to memory.

What Dexter knew and what was not in her personnel file, was that she had a photographic memory. All she had to do was to read or see something once and it was stamped into her subconscious. Hence the reason she was so good at her analytic job, deep in the bowels of headquarters.

Ping! The lifts doors hissed open, and Dexter got in. The smell of disinfectant stung her nostrils. She pressed the button for the basement. The doors hissed closed and the cubical jerked slightly as it began to descend.

A few minutes later, the doors hissed open again and Dexter got out. There was a sign suspended from thin wires from the roof directing her to the various departments that inhabited this forgotten realm. Ahead was her destination – the armoury section but to her right was the archives. She decided to take a detour and headed right.

"Yes?" Asked a small woman sitting behind a light-coloured wooden table. Her spectacles perched precariously on the end of her nose. "Can I help you?"

"World War Two."

"1939 – 1945." Snapped back the woman. "Six years. Need to be more specific." The woman's green eyes glared at Dexter over the top of her spectacles like the fabled Medusa trying to turn the young operative to stone.

"Operation Dionysus."

"Third row. Halfway down." Informed the woman. Dexter started to walk in the direction of the row upon row of shelves, when the woman added, "...under the letter 'D'."

The addition made Dexter glared back at her with a '*do you think I stupid?*' look on her face but the show of defiance was lost on the woman because she had her head buried in a book. After a lot of searching, despite the rather cryptic directions she had been given, Dexter found the file see had been looking for.

It was several inches thick and covered in dust. She found an empty table at the back of the room and dropped it down on to the table with a thud, which seemed to echo off the walls, causing the woman at the entrance to look up once more from her book and fire a disapproving look in Dexter's direction.

Click! Went the small reading light that was the only thing, apart from the file, that was on the table. Dexter pulled a metal fold-up chair along the floor, its legs making a scrapping sound as she did so, causing another look from the woman. Dexter mouthed her apologises and then settled down to read what was in the file. She was a fast reader and skimmed through the pages like a wildfire through dry undergrowth.

The Germans had indeed used chemical enhancements to aid their troops during the conflict. According to the intelligence reports, it went from the Wehrmacht (the German Army) all the way up to Hitler himself. She read:

'The use of methamphetamines, better known as crystal meth, was particularly prevalent: a pill form of the drug, Pervitin, was distributed by the millions to Wehrmacht units before the successful invasion of France in 1940.'

'Developed by the Temmler pharmaceutical company, Pervitin was introduced in 1938 and marketed as a magic pill for alertness and an anti-depressive, among other uses. It was briefly even available over the counter for the mass, in other words, the German people....'

"Jesus!" Exclaimed Dexter, her eyes wide with shock at what she was reading. She continued.

'...*a military doctor, Otto Ranke, experimented with Pervitin on 90 college students and decided, based on his results, that the drug would help Germany win the war. Using Pervitin, the soldiers of the Wehrmacht could stay awake for days at a time and march many more miles without resting.*'

'*A so-called 'stimulant decree' issued in April 1940, sent more than 35 million tablets of Pervitin and Isophan (a slightly modified version produced by the Knoll pharmaceutical company) of the pills to the front lines, where they fuelled the Nazis' 'Blitzkrieg' ('Lightning War') invasion of France through the Ardennes mountains.*'

'*It should be noted that the Germans were not alone in their use of performance-enhancing drugs during World War Two. Allied soldiers were known to use amphetamines (speed) in the form of Benzedrine to battle combat fatigue.*'

Dexter let out a low whistle, stunned by what she had just read. She briefly looked at the rest of the file, which droned on about the use of chemical stimulants and the Nazis hierarchy but that did not interest her. All she wanted to know was the reasoning behind '*Operation Dionysus*' and she had found it.

With the Germans exaggerated up to high doh on Pervitin, no wonder the Allies wanted to stop the manufacturing of the drug, and going by what she had already read in the Dionysus file mission report, the attack had been a mixed bag when it came to the outcome.

The commandos, led by Fuller, after a brief skirmish with some Italian troops garrisoned in a nearby village, had found the factory in Greece empty, void of any trace of the chemicals they were looking for. That was the minus side of the operation.

On the plus side, however, they had found sufficient intelligence on the major players in the manufacturing of the drugs to produce a '*hit-list*' which would be used later, either for elimination or to '*poach*' the scientists across to the Allies once the war had ended, as in another more famous operation – '*Operation Paperclip*.'

The telephone on the desk where the woman sat rang. She answered it. Spoke briefly ending the conversation with a nod of her head before replacing the handset. She turned in Dexter's direction and yelled, "Are you Miss Dexter?"

Dexter nodded.

"That was upstairs calling…they're wondering where the hell you are, to put it bluntly."

Dexter looked at her watch. Shit! She had had her nose buried in those files for over an hour. She hurriedly pushed the sheets of paper together like a very bad croupier trying to shuffle an oversized pack of cards whilst her customers looked on. Pages moved in opposite directions to each other, suddenly gaining minds of their own.

Uncooperative and downright frustrating. She would push and one sheet would fall to the floor. She would bend down to retrieve the wayward page, stand up and then knock the corner of the folder, sending an avalanche of pages sliding across the desk, with only a mad panicky lunge from her saving them from toppling off the end of the table.

Dexter heard the clickity-clack of metal upon concrete, and she turned her head to her left, remaining spread-eagled on the desktop. It was the woman from the front desk. A smile upon her face, whether Dexter predicament had thawed her icy exterior or she had reconsidered, is still open for debate, but the woman placed a hand on Dexter's back.

"I'll get this, dearie. Think it's time you weren't here." Suggested the woman. Dexter got up slowly and smiled back at her. She left the archives and headed towards the armoury, at double quick time, pushing through the double doors, and it was like Alice entering Wonderland for the very first time.

In front of her were rows of benches with people in lab coats busily working at them. This was the armoury department, later to be changed to the equipment section, run by Robert '*Sparks*' Cuthbertson. Robert had replaced his father Gerald, when he retired, and had been in the position since the late nineties, around the same time James Scott took over control.

He lives with his partner Lynda, and their three children, all married with children of their own. She found him busy at one of the benches staring down the lenses of a microscope, deep in conversation with another lab technician. He was so engrossed in the conversation that Dexter had to cough to get his attention.

"Yes?" He barked.

"Fiona Dexter."

"Who?"

"That's me. I've been ordered to report to you to be issued with my firearm."

He clicked his tongue on the roof of his mouth and rolled his eyes. Murmuring his displeasure under his breath he walked across to a rack full of distinct types of weapons. Everything from automatic pistols to grenade launchers to assault rifles of several types.

"Those are all to be destroyed." He said noticing Dexter's eye light up like a child in a candy store. "The operational ones are through here." He took her into another room, this time with a cage. He pressed a code into the keypad and the door clicked open. She followed him in.

Cuthbertson handed her a manila-coloured piece of paper. "Fill this out and sign it." He reached into his left breast pocket and pulled out a pen. She looked at it warily.

"For goodness' sake. It's a pen! It writes and doesn't explode or release poison gas!"

He clicked his tongue again, murmured some kind of profanity under his breath and then disappeared out of sight for a moment behind a stack of shelves, before returning carrying a small black automatic. He handed it to Dexter.

"Walther PPK. Seven point six-five millimetre with a delivery like a brick through a plate glass window." He smiled at his private joke.

He had heard that phrase in a movie and had always wanted to say it at his place of work. "In other words, dearie, point it at the bad guy and pull the trigger."

He retrieved the signed paperwork, and went back through to the main room, where he picked up a leather shoulder holster from one of the vacant benches. "Try this."

He almost threw it at her.

"It has adjustable sliders, for you to make it fit more snuggly." And that was his final word, he shuffled off back to the bench he had been at when Dexter had arrived. She stood there stunned. A young blonde-haired woman in a lab coat walked past.

"Don't worry about him. He speaks to all the females like that."

"What an asshole!"

"Yip. That's what you get when you go old school."

"Still no excuse. This is the twenty-first century not the Middle Ages."

"Down here, Cuthbertson's law rules. Get used to it."

And this was why, three hours later, she was sitting in a car outside Fuller's father's house, just as the mystery man left after leaving Fuller lying on the floor. She quickly took a couple of photographs of the mystery man before starting her car engine and slowly following him at a safe distance.

Eventually, the mystery man got into a black sedan, and she lost it in the traffic but not before mentally noting the licence plate. She would check on that later.

By the time she returned to Fuller's father's house, the police were already there investigating a noise complaint from a neighbour. She thought better of it advertising her presence, so she drove past and away. She stopped the car in a public car park and switched the engine off. Her heart was racing.

She tried to control her breathing, but her eyes kept darting up at her rear-view mirror, which made things worse, so she got out of the car and started walking.

The cold briskness of the air momentarily took her breath away, which snapped her back into professional mode. Her phone buzzed. There was a result on the images she had taken.

Otto Werner. Current employment unknown. She scrolled the screen up. *Current whereabouts unknown. Wanted in conjunction with two alleged murders and three assaults.*

She started to hyperventilate again and grabbed onto a metal bench to stop herself from collapsing.

"Are you alright luv?" Inquired an old lady walking her dog.

"Fine thanks. Just found out my boyfriend's two timing me." Dexter lied.

"The bastard! Take a tip from an old pro Luv – cut his balls off when you get the chance!" And with her free hand, the old woman simulated a chopping action before yanking at her dog's chain and moving off, cackling like a witch as she went.

Dexter laughed. "I'll take that under advisement." She walked back to her car and drove home. Home for Fiona Dexter was a one bedroomed flat above a Chinese restaurant.

Mr. Wu, the owner, was a kindly old gentleman, who had taken pity on the young woman that had turned up in response to the newspaper advert for a tenant for his flat above his restaurant. The '*student*' looked half-starved when she arrived so, from that day onwards, he always made sure some food was delivered upstairs to 'feed her up.'

At first, he was slightly concerned about the odd hours his tenant was keeping but he soon got used to the idea. The entrance to her flat was via an alley that ran along the right side of the restaurant '*The Golden Dragon.*' Entry was restricted thanks to a keypad next to the bottom door. She pressed the six-figure number and went in, being careful to close it behind her.

Walked up a flight of thirteen stairs to get to the flat door, and there on the floor waiting for her was a plastic bag with some delicious aromas coming from it. A small note was attached with a simple message on it scrawled in pencil – '*Eat. W.*' She smiled contentedly as, once again, her guardian angel had read her thoughts. She took the meal and went in.

7 – Alison White to See...

Dexter unpacked the meal and laid it out on a white plastic tray. She rescued a fork and spoon from the drawer next to the sink, placed them on the tray and then took them over to her three-seater couch. Time for some mood music, she thought.

"Alexa, play I get a kick out of you..."

"Playing I get a kick out of you by Frank Sinatra." The first bars of the tune started.

"Alexa, stop!" Yelled Dexter, annoyed at her lack of clarity with the smart speaker. "Play, I get a kick out of you by Emma Smith."

"Playing, I get I kick out of you by Emma Smith." The tune started to play. The dulcet tones of the female vocalist a far cry from the velvetiness of the original but her choice in music help to sum Dexter up. She liked to be a rebel. Try something different, hence her choice in this singer.

As she devoured her meal, Dexter flicked through the file Scott had given her. Nothing really stood out or added to the knowledge she had about the mission except for the last two pages. Something sparked her interest. The coroner's report on colonel Eric James Fuller reported that he had had a heart attack. She looked at the breakdown of the report and shook her head. There was also a report from a Robert Jenkins.

This was a police interview and Jenkins was one of Fuller's closest friends. In the report, he expressed his shock at the sudden passing of his friend and his regrets that his son Gregor had not been informed.

Dexter scrambled for something to write on, eventually, finding a notepad and pencil. She scribbled down Jenkins' name and address, putting a large question mark next to him. She made a mental note to visit Jenkins tomorrow.

The second thing that caught her eye was the phrase 'Das Wolfsrudel.' It was obviously German. She picked up her phone and googled the meaning. It instantly came back with 'The Wolfpack.' Another question mark only, larger. She also noted down Johannes Riga and Falcone Industries underlining each several times.

She stretched and yawned as the mixture of the warm food and lack of sleep ganged up on her. She left the notes, folder, and half empty food cartons where they lay and went through to her modest bedroom.

Took off her shoulder holster, tossed it on a chair and flopped on to the bed. She was asleep before her head hit the pillow.

Dexter slept soundly. Usually, she tossed and turned as her brain tried to digest the day's information but that night, a calm came upon her which, when she woke, troubled her. She showered, had breakfast – toast and a black coffee – and put on a towelling robe and used a towel to dry her hair.

She picked up her mobile and dialled the number for Robert Jenkins that she had scribbled down on her note pad the previous night. After four rings, a man's voice answered.

"Hello?"

"Mr. Jenkins. Mr. Robert Jenkins?"

"Yes."

"Hello, sir. My name is Alison White. I'm a freelance reporter and doing a story on your friend, the late Eric Fuller..."

"Aye and..."

"I'm looking into his wartime exploits, and I was wondering if I could speak to you about and get a general feeling what kind of man he was."

"Well, I'm playing golf at one this afternoon. If you can get to the Eagleton Golf club before I tee-off, I might be able to tell you a few things."

"I can be there for twelve fifteen, if that would be okay?"

"Fine. See you there, lassie."

"See you then, Mr. Jenkins." She pressed the cancel button on her phone.

For the first time in a while, Dexter felt pleased with herself. She did not feel guilty about lying to Jenkins because that came with the job, but she needed to remember to keep up the façade while she was in his presence. She went through to the bedroom and opened her wardrobe. '*What would a budding journalist wear?*' She thought as she searched through the hangers.

She emerged fifteen minutes later wearing a pale blouse, charcoal grey skirt that barely reached her knees, black flat shoes, and a charcoal grey jacket. The jacket served two purposes – firstly she felt more empowered wearing it and secondly and more important, it hid the shoulder holster containing the Walther.

She reached into a drawer next to her couch and picked up a set of circular rimmed glasses with false lenses, grabbed a couple of pens and a new pad from the drawer, before closing it.

The drive to the Eagleton golf club was pleasurable, as the sun shone through the windscreen of her car, a sliver-coloured Fiat Punto. She wound down the window and allowed herself time to relax, as she leaned her right elbow on the door, whilst gripping the wheel with her left hand.

She slowed to a stop at a set of traffic lights that turned red as she approached. The pause gave her just enough time to reach down and switch on her car stereo. Instantly some kind of noise blared from the speakers found on the boot shelf behind her.

She turned the volume down, so it went from scarily loud, to background music, the kind you would hear if you were standing in an elevator, going between floors in a major department store. The lights changed and she moved off. She even allowed herself to tap along to the music.

She turned left and started up the gravel drive that took her to the Eagleton golf and country club or that is what the large green and white sign promised that she drove past. She looked at her watch as she pulled up in front of a large stately home.

As she parked the car and got out, she almost expected some kind of footman or even a butler to come out, carrying a silver tray with flutes filled with champagne, and in a posh accent, offer her one.

Too many period dramas on the television, Dex. Retrieving her shoulder bag from the passenger seat, containing her notepad and pen, as well as a small dictaphone, slung it over her shoulder and locked the car. She thought through her cover story to remind herself, as she began to climb the six stone steps that took her to the main door. As she entered the reception area it was like she had been transported back in time.

The sheer decadence of the interior of the building was a sight to be seen. There were oil paintings on the walls that Dexter assumed were past members of the club.

The floor was ice-rink standard of polished. There was a pine tree freshness about the air. All staff members wore a uniform complete with name badge.

Black trousers, black shoes, a scarlet waist coat, black tie with the club crest on it and a crisp white blouse / shirt all except the gentleman who made his way across the floor to greet her.

He wore a scarlet blazer instead of the waistcoat with the club crest on his left breast pocket. His name badge, unlike the others which bore their first names, informed each visitor that this was Mr. Jackson. To Dexter, he reminded her of a throwback to the old stately houses and the head butler.

"Can I help you, madam?"

"Miss Alison White to see Mr. Stephen Jenkins."

"Ah yes. Mr. Jenkins is in the Player's Lounge. If you would follow me, please." He motioned with his left hand the direction he wanted Dexter to go before heading that way, with her a few steps behind. They went through a large wooden panelled doorway into another room that was decked out just as fine as the earlier one, but now the air had changed to the smell of alcohol and cigar smoke.

The smell made her feel momentarily queasy, but she swallowed hard to try and keep it under control. With that and the fact there was a pterodactyl doing hand stands in her stomach, added to the feeling that Scott had chosen the wrong person for this assignment, as she felt that she was in the deep end of a swimming pool, the lifeguard not noticing she was drowning.

She was escorted to a table where a man was seated sipping on a glass of golden liquid. He stood up as she approached. "Mr. Jenkins, this is Miss White." Introduced Jackson. Jenkins extended a hand and the two shook before sitting down. Jackson hovered.

"A drink?" Asked Jenkins.

"Fruit juice please." Jenkins lifted a quizzical eyebrow. "I'm driving." He nodded his approval placing his hand over his glass signifying to Jackson he was not requiring a refill.

"One fruit juice." Repeated Jackson and left. Dexter pretended to fumble in her shoulder bag for her notepad and pen. She was not acting too hard, she was petrified. After what seemed like an age, she found it and got herself comfortable in her chair, crossing her right leg over left.

"How can I help you, Miss White?" Jackson appeared with her drink, placed it in front of her and left. Jenkins reached forward and picked up his drink. "Whisky. Nothing beats a single malt before a round."

Jenkins was a smallish man around five foot five, Dexter would later estimate. Brown hair styled in the classic 'short back and sides' style. Full of face and of stomach too. '*Too many pies.*' Dexter thought but there was something striking that caught her eye, at once.

As Jenkins had leaned forward to get his drink, she noticed a tattoo on his left wrist that consisted of numbers and letters. The puzzled look on her face did not go unnoticed and Jenkins followed her gaze down to his arm.

"Och!" He dismissed in his broad Scottish accent, "I see you've spotted my body art. A foolish mistake when I was in the army. It's my birth date and my blood type in case I was wounded in battle."

He pulled the sleeve of his jumper over it.

Over the next half an hour, the two talked about the war and Fuller's participation in it, what was not classified anyway.

Jenkins came across as quite a confident man not short of embellishing some of his wartime exploits, to please his captive audience. All through the interview, Dexter scribbled down some notes, mostly for show as her mind was 'recording' everything.

"Will you excuse me?" She said getting to her feet, Jenkins rose too. "Can you tell me where the ladies' room is? I need to powder my nose." Jenkins directed her to the nearest toilet and watched her leave.

He put a hand in his trouser pocket and pulled out a small plastic envelope with a zip top. Pulled back the seal, sprinkling some of the contents, a white powder, into Dexter's drink before closing the envelope and returning it to his pocket. He took out his mobile and input a number.

"It's Jenkins. We've got a problem. I need you to bring the car round to the front of the club, in ten minutes." He closed his phone just as Dexter returned. "Would you believe it my opponent has just called to cancel."

"I'm so sorry." Apologised Dexter, "I hope it wasn't anything to do with me?" She sat down and took a mouthful from her drink.

"No. No. Something came up at his firm and he's had to reschedule. Anyway, it gives us more time to chat." Jenkins sat back in his chair and waited. After a few minutes, he noticed that his little addition to Dexter's drink, was starting to take effect. It took her two attempts to pick up her glass, the second time she went for a drink. She got to her feet and staggered.

"Whoa!" She exclaimed grabbing the arm of her chair. Jenkins reached over and grabbed her arm to stop her falling forwards.

"What kind of juice did they give her? I don't feel so good." And with that, she almost folded herself back into the chair. Jenkins reached over and checked her pulse on her wrist. Steady. It was then he realised he was not alone. A tall thin man in a pale suit stood beside him.

"What have you done?" Asked the newcomer. "You were told to feed her minimal information and that was all!" The irritation in the newcomer's voice was plain to hear.

"She was asking too many questions, and she noticed my tattoo. What else could I do?" Defended Jenkins.

"You were told to conceal that." Reminded the newcomer referring to the tattoo.

"I wear it with pride."

"You are an outdated fool!" Cursed the newcomer grabbing one of Dexter's arms as Jenkins grabbed the other. A couple of the other members looked over. "My friend's just had too much to drink. We're taking her to her taxi."

The onlookers accepted this explanation and returned to what they were doing. They looped Dexter's arms around their necks as they took her to the main door and down the steps to the awaiting 'taxi' which turned out to be a dark coloured Mercedes.

The newcomer held onto the limp body of Dexter whilst Jenkins opened the rear passenger door. They both laid her gently in the back and closed the door. The newcomer got in the driver's side whilst Jenkins got in the front passenger. They drove off down the driveway past a Ford with one person inside.

The Mercedes drove out of the city and along various country roads before ending up at a deserted farmhouse. It pulled up and stopped. Both men manhandled Dexter into the front room and sat her down on a chair.

While Jenkins tied her up, the newcomer went out and surveyed the surroundings. Satisfied no-one had followed them, he returned to the main room of the house and rechecked Dexter's pulse. Steady. He took out his mobile phone and pressed in a number. After two rings a woman's voice answered.

"Verification?"

"Alpha-two-nine-control."

"Confirmed. Transferring you…"

"This is control. Report." Said a man's voice with a heavy French accent.

"Operation mis-lead has failed."

"How?"

"Number nine has compromised the mission by abducting the reporter."

"I see." Came back the short but cold reply. "Your suggestion on how to remedy this, number twenty-nine?"

"Termination of both."

"Agreed." The phone went dead. Twenty-nine put away his phone and walked over to the unconscious Dexter and frisked her. He found the bulge in her jacket and reached in and pulled out the automatic.

He raised a puzzled eyebrow. Jenkins came back into the room and his usually calm face changed to a look of shock when he saw what his partner was holding.

"A Walther PPK. Don't seem to remember the press being allocated with weapons."

"But twenty-nine...I didn't know." Pleaded Jenkins holding his hands out in a failed attempt at reconciliation.

"If she is armed, then she must be with one of the security services." Surmised twenty-nine. "You bloody fool!" He raised his hand to strike Jenkins but stopped. "Pick her up and we'll take her into the woods and dispose of her."

Wiping the torrent of sweat from his forehead, Jenkins nodded compliance and untied Dexter. Between the two of them, they manhandled the limp body of Dexter out of the car and into the woods.

Two hours later, Dexter was awakened by a repeated pain on her face. Someone was slapping her. She instinctively put her hands up to defend herself as she opened her eyes to see who was doing this.

"Hello Dex." Greeted a familiar face grinning down at her. She pushed the man away and sat up.

"Fallon."

"Were you expecting someone else?" Asked the man with a wry smile on his face.

"What the hell are you doing here and where is here?" She looked around still dazed.

"The colonel asked me to check up on you, and I followed you to the country club. I was about to walk in on you when I noticed two men carrying you to their car.

Knowing that you're not '*that*' kind of girl I decided to follow them."

"Must admit, I got a bit worried when they lifted you out of the car and took you into the woods." He smiled and sauntered over to a table where a decanter was sitting along with several glasses.

"Drink?" He asked hovering the decanter over an empty glass. She shook her head. "Anyway, I parked the car," he continued as he poured himself two fingers worth of whisky, "and decided to follow them. Glad I did though, as one of them was about to put a hole in the back of your head."

Dexter motioned to the drinks table and Fallon poured her a drink. She downed it in one. "Needless to say, our two friends won't be bothering us again." She went to the table and poured herself another.

"Steady, Dex. The colonel wants to see us and I'd rather you walked in and not have me carry you." She glared at him but took on board what he had said and put the glass down.

"Bathroom?" Fallon pointed to a blue door off to the right.

"I've got some spare clothes in the wardrobe in the bedroom that might fit."

"Whatever." Came the reply from the other side of the bathroom door as Fallon heard the shower. Before Dexter stepped into the shower, she smelled herself. Yip, something did smell, and it was her!

8 – Desk Job

After a brief shower and a change of clothes – jeans, trainers, and a checked shirt – Dexter and Fallon made their way back to headquarters and a reckoning with colonel Scott.

Dexter noted as they entered the office's outer sanctum that there was no-one at the secretary's desk. Fallon knocked on the door.

"Enter!"

The two operatives came in. Fallon left Dexter to close the door and then both stood at stiff attention. Scott ignored them and continued to read a memo in front of him. He picked up a pen, scribbled his signature at the bottom, put the pen back, placing the memo in his out tray, before looking at them with a look that would melt ice.

"Operation shattered truth is a shambles!" He began, "one of our oldest operatives is dead, and now I hear a further two men have been found dead in some wood, not far from being seen leaving with a rather worst for wear, Miss Dexter."

"They drugged me, sir." Said Dexter trying to defend herself. "If it wasn't for K-12, they're would have been another body found in the woods." She looked across at Fallon and flashed him a brief nervous smile.

"Then it was a good job I sent him to clean up this mess!"

"To be fair, sir…" Began Fallon.

"I should be blaming myself for selecting you for this mission. A rookie operative…"

"With all due respect, sir. We all have to start somewhere." Suggested Fallon. But almost crumbled under the glare from his superior.

"Enough." Snapped Scott like he was scolding an unruly puppy. "Have we learned anything?" He scanned both of them. Dexter replied.

"The man seen coming out of Fuller's house was an Otto Werner. A Neo-Nazi with links to various far right groups." Scott put his hands together making his index fingers into a point and resting his chin on them. "I would bet my career on it, that if we did a check on the two men that abducted and tried to kill me, we would find a link back to Werner."

"Miss Dexter."

"Sir."

"A word of advice. Don't make bets your body can't cash."

"She does have a valid point, sir." Defended Fallon.

"I've already had intelligence look into those two men. They are linked to an organisation called 'The Wolf Pack' and someone called Viktor Titus. I've asked 'I' Section to investigate. Anything else?"

"I did notice that Jenkins had a strange tattoo on his left forearm. When I asked him, he got quite defensive dismissing it as an old army tattoo."

"Interesting." Scott wrote something down on a note pad he had in front of him. "I'll get intelligence to look into that. In the meantime, I want you to look into this Riga person." Dexter nodded and turned to leave. "Where are you going, Miss Dexter?"

"To do as you've suggested, sir and look into Titus."

"Not you." He ordered. "K-12, that's your assignment. I also want you to check out the disappearance of Fuller's only son – Gregor. No one's seen him since the incident at his father's house."

Fallon nodded and left. "Miss Dexter," he continued, "you may have noticed that my front office was vacant one person." Dexter nodded.

"I'm afraid Mrs. Robertson has been taken unwell, and I need a replacement as soon as possible. In retrospect, you were right, a few days ago, when you said you're not a field operative."

"Therefore, as of tomorrow, I'm putting your talents to more effective uses as my personal assistant with no drop in pay or rank." Dexter opened her mouth to complain but was shut down at once by a look from Scott. "Dismissed."

Dexter exited the office and stared at the vacant desk, her new assignment as of tomorrow. She felt like a deflated balloon. Her morale had gone, from being at the top of the waterslide, to the messy splashing and regaining your feet at the bottom.

Scott was right.

She had been promoted too early and had a lot to learn. However, she had not been sacked but been given a second chance as his personal assistant and she was not going to let him down. She would show him - hell, she would show the world!

Meanwhile, behind the protection of the large wooden door, Scott was standing looking out his office window at the hustle and bustle of life in the capital. He envied those anonymous faces who had such carefree lives with no clue of the dirtier nastier side of human nature. He sighed, before walking over to his desk and sitting down.

He looked down at the file in front of him, sighed again, shook his head, and closed it. '*Pencil pusher.*' He thought as he opened a drawer in his desk, tossed the folder in it and closed it again. He missed the excitement of 'the game.' Espionage. Good versus Evil.

The mind games of having to out-think your opponent with the satisfaction of the result of being able to go home knowing you had saved the world from itself. Now all he does is look at files, press buttons on a computer screen and assign nameless people to assignments that may end up with them being killed.

His operatives were nothing but names, either in a file or on the memorial wall, which greeted you as you entered the building.

It made him sick but if it was not him doing it, some other desk jockey would be. He hated getting old. His right hand reached down and opened the bottom drawer of his desk, brought out a bottle of whisky, a clean glass, unscrewed the top on the bottle, poured a decent measure of the liquid into the glass and place the bottle on the desktop.

He picked up the glass and swirled the golden liquid around thoughtfully before taking a sip. It slid down his throat like a velvet glove moving across glass. Another sip, before putting the glass down, and reached for the telephone. Dialled an internal number and let it ring. After several rings, a man's voice answered and requested which extension.

"Two-one-four."

"Hold please." There were a couple of clicks on the line. Scott assumed this was the operator connecting him. Another voice came on, female this time.

"Department one."

"This is Scott. K-Section. '*Operation Shattered Truth*' is still operational. Assignment changed to a different officer."

"Understood."

"Please inform '*The Committee*' that I don't appreciate their interference in my section's day to day operations."

"A message will be passed upstairs. Anything else sir?"

"Yes. If they interfere again, I will be handing in my notice!" And with that, he slammed the telephone down. Feeling better about himself, he took a long-lasting gulp of whisky, emptying his glass, before returning the bottle and glass to the safety of the bottom drawer.

The next morning, after a less than peaceful sleep, Fiona Dexter took her place behind the desk in Scott's outer office. She logged into the computer, moved a few things on the desktop, and searched through the drawers, binning anything suspicious or not needed.

Reaching into her bag, she pulled out a name plate with her name on it (she had been handed this as she exited the building by the security officer on the front desk) and placed it in front of her – announcing Miss F. Dexter had arrived, all but a roundabout route.

She took off her jacket and hung it on the back of her chair, revealing her shoulder holster and her automatic. She took the holster off, opened one of the lower drawers, put it in, then closed and lock the drawer. She finally stretched her arms out to the side, yawned, and gave herself a shake just as the outer door opened, Scott walked in, carrying a coffee cup and a newspaper tucked under his arm. He nodded to Dexter.

"Morning Miss Dexter." He said as he walked past.

"Morning sir." The inner door closed.

9 – Fallon

Jacob Fallon, or 'Jake' to his friends, was an intelligence officer with over a decade's worth of experience and seven years in the military before that. He was the great grandson of Jonathan Fallon, a legend in OSP circles, and liked to visit the family home, Ashton Manor, as often as he could. His mother,

Molly, now in her late sixties, still stayed there enjoying her retirement surrounded by pictures and memories.

A large portrait of Jonathan now hung in the main hall. The manor house itself had been extensively redesigned over the years, with an extension added to the back of the building, several of the outbuildings had turned into holiday cottages, adding extra income to the property. Although Jake has never married, his sister Stephanie Isabella did. Ruben Michel, a French banker.

Their union bore fruit giving Molly three grandchildren – Louise, Amy, and Laura. All red heads like their mother and grandmother. Molly still enjoyed long walks near the Manor, like she did as a child with her father, Peter.

Amongst the many mementos and pictures, is a possession she cherishes above all else – it sits in a glass covered bookcase in her study, where she sits and writes children's stories.

It is a first edition of a book entitled '*The Animal Tea-Party*,' written by Robyn Smythe, a friend of the family, signed and gifted to her on her sixtieth birthday.

The reason that this book is so special to her, is that it is the story her grandfather, or '*Pops*,' told her one stormy night, way back when she was a little girl of nine. It was a nonsense story about jungle animals who have a tea-party. It was silly but it made her feel safe.

That nothing would ever harm her. As she grew into a young lady, Molly would visit her aging relative and eventually manage to get him to recall the story, which she jotted down and sent to an inspiring author friend who was looking for a story to launch his new career.

Every time Molly feels down and depressed, she would take the book out and read it quietly to herself or if the grandchildren came for a visit, she would sit them down and read. Next to the book, propped up on a cushion, was a gold lighter with the Fallon crest and motto emblazoned on it – 'Non Est Optio Defectum.' Which meant – 'Failure isn't an option.'

This credo has been instilled in all the Fallon line from Jonathan to Peter and then Molly. Each branch of the tree took it upon themselves to train their offspring in all aspects of the espionage game just in case they would follow in the 'family' business. Jonathan started it, training Peter from an early age, after what happened when members of the Falcone family kidnapped Molly-Beth, his wife, and the baby Peter.

Molly-Beth was working for the Office of Special Projects when she met the dashing young army major in Cairo during the second year of the Great War, that she would eventually fall in love with, and marry.

She would later retire from the OSP to settle down to raise Peter and become a schoolteacher, but she would never forget her training, actively taking part in Peter's training when he was able.

Peter would continue the tradition joining the OSP at the outbreak of the Second War, distinguishing himself during many classified operations. He would meet and marry Victoria Aymes in Nineteen Forty-Two and Molly would be born a couple of years later.

She relished coming to the country and staying at Ashton Manor in the Summer holidays. She loved listening to Pops' stories of daring do and even some of his sillier ones.

He was a very bubbly individual, but his demeanour would change if you asked him about the war or his life before settling down at the Manor. It went from bubbly to dark and sombre.

It reminded Molly of what happened when you opened a lemonade bottle and allowed the fizz to escape. One minute you had bubbles then next flat lemon flavoured liquid.

She was academically gifted and did well in her subjects, eventually going to university to study childcare. She graduated with honours and went on to become a teacher, like her mother. In the mid-sixties, when she was in her early twenties, she met and fell in love with George Wilson, a captain in the army.

There was even talk of marriage and they were engaged in November 1975 with plans to get married the following year. More good news followed when Molly found out she was expecting which delighted all concerned.

She decided to have the baby, which turned out to be twins, Jacob, and Stephanie, having them in June the following year. George was absent from the birth, as he was away on secondment and could not get leave. He had managed to put in for leave in September, however, fate through a spanner in the works when Robert was sent to Vietnam and was killed in action in March.

Molly was devastated but her family intervened sending her off to the Isle of Mull to recover from her loss and this was where the twins grew up, surrounded by loving relatives.

10 – *Mister Whitestone*

Fallon liked to keep himself physically fit by running most mornings along the shore that bordered where he stayed. He also like the gym and swimming. He was in his forties and sometimes, his body made him feel older. He was five foot ten inches in height, with short brown hair, and a medium build. It took him four years to earn his 'K' designation and he was proud of it. Killing was not part of his nature, yet he would without hesitation, if the need arose.

The thing he liked about working for the Office of Special Projects, was they allowed their operatives free reign when it came to the choice of their personal weapon. Fallon liked the Walther and used it as his back-up weapon, but his primary choice was a Walther P-38, it was not a compact as the PPK but it held an eight round clip instead of six, which he thought gave him a slight edge.

After the awkward dressing down both he and Dexter had received from Scott, he had gone home and soaked in a cold shower contemplating both what had just happened, and what was about to come. After his shower, he sat in front of his laptop with a towel wrapped around his waist covering his modesty. He entered his personal log in code and went through the various security levels until he reached what he wanted.

He typed in a request for information on his current assignment and only had to wait a few seconds before the required information came up. Using his mouse, he scanned through it page by page familiarising himself with the details.

After a couple of hours of both digesting the files and feeling guilty about the way Dexter had been treated, he got dressed and headed back to the office but this time it was down to the armoury section.

As he walked in, the usual smell of a mixture of gun oil and gunpowder greeted him.

"Ah, K-12. How nice to see you again." It was Cuthbertson. The equipment officer extended a friendly hand. They shook. "So glad they've assigned you to this operation rather than that child." The disdain in Cuthbertson's voice was plain to hear. It was like he had swallowed one of those sour sweets and it was sourer than he had expected but was too polite to spit it out. Fallon glared at him.

"Miss Dexter is new to the role." He said trying to defend his colleague.

"But still…"

"No buts! Everybody must start somewhere. I know that you thought I was some jumped up asshole when I joined the service!"

Fallon was almost yelling now, and this brought concerned looks from the other people on the floor. He lowered his voice a little, as the two men walked.

Everyone that was there could tell Cuthbertson was both flustered by Fallon's outburst and surprised. "If I hear you've been discourteous to another member of staff, male or female, then I will report you. Do I make myself clear?" Cuthbertson gave a sheepish nod. The two men stopped at a workbench full of equipment. Cuthbertson reached over and picked up a watch.

"What does this do?"

"Mainly it tells the time." Said Cuthbertson trying but not lightening the mood. "It also has a homing beacon in it which is activated when you press the stopwatch and time button simultaneously." Fallon took off his own watch and put on the new one.

"And like my father used to say, the winder does more than keep good time. It can also shorten someone's time on this earth if you get my meaning?" A phone rang and moments later, one of the other lab-coated staff came across.

"That was the colonel on the line, sir." He said speaking to Fallon. "You are needed back upstairs urgently." Fallon thanked all present and went to the left.

When he re-entered Scott's office, Fallon found his superior and Dexter watching a news report about a body being found somewhere in Scotland. He was about to ask what was happening but was stopped by Scott who pointed at the screen.

"This is Katrina Anderson, reporting from the Clyde Valley, where the body of a man has been retrieved from the river. The Police are not releasing any details now until the victim's family have been notified. Back to you in the studio."

Scott switched off the television and turned to Fallon and Dexter.

"His name was Robert Foster..." Scott said with a tinge of sadness in his voice.

"Who was, sir?" Asked Dexter.

"The body they pulled out of the Clyde."

"Ah."

"He worked as an analyst for us. He was supposed to be on vacation, but I received a call from him just before he left, telling me that he had stumbled upon something that I needed to see."

"Did you ever find out what he had found, sir?" Asked Fallon.

"No. He did, however, say that he had sent a copy to James Fuller and also had a back-up copy hidden away for my eyes only."

"Seems a bit paranoid to me, sir." Suggested Fallon.

"I don't like coincidences K-12. First, Fuller dying suddenly, then his son disappearing, and now Foster..."

"I see your point, sir."

"I am putting '*Operation Shattered Truth*' on hold until further notice. I want you to get up to Scotland and do some digging into Foster's death."

"Very good, sir." Fallon went to leave.

"Sparks is waiting for you outside the building with something that will get you there fast."

"Sir."

Fallon retraced his steps through security, finishing with signing himself out. He handed back his identification badge to the guard at the front desk before exiting the building via the automatic doors. True to form, Cuthbertson was waiting for him leaning on the bonnet of a fast-looking sports car.

Fallon recognised the badge on the bonnet – Aston Martin. He was blown away.

"Meet the Aston Martin V12 Vantage. Five hundred and sixty-three break horsepower, with a top speed of 205 miles per hour."

"Any special modifications?" Asked Fallon hoping.

"This is the real world, K-12. You're not James bloody Bond!" Snapped an irritated Cuthbertson. "What is it with all you youngsters these days, wanting exploding pens and cars that fire missiles. It just doesn't happen."

He opened the driver's door and ushered Fallon inside handing him the keys as the operative took his place. Fallon turned the engine over and at once; he could feel the power as the engine roared like some caged beast.

His eyes lit up and he licked his lips. The same way a young child acts at Christmas when they receive their dream gift. "Take great care of this piece of equipment and obey the highway code." And with that, Cuthbertson slammed the door shut, allowing Fallon to speed off into the afternoon traffic.

The Aston Martin turned left following the signs to the New Mill Hotel several long boring hours later. He could do with a shower, and something to eat, but the mission came first. The car slowly pulled around the bends heading down towards his destination. A slow left, a tight right until he came to the bottom.

Apart from the modern cars parked outside some of the houses, it was like stepping back in time. Various members of staff in period costumes mingled with tourist while others posed for photographs.

A man dress in costume, wearing a chimney style top hat, also posed for pictures, and pointed people in the right direction. Fallon turned right. Then at the bottom of the road, the Hotel emerged from behind the trees like it had been playing hide and seek with him.

He found a vacant parking spot and got out. He stretched and yawned. He wished he had taken a flight up to the airport and then driven the hour or so to the site but as the saying goes, hindsight is a wonderful thing.

He opened one of the glass doors, which had a relief of the Hotel etched on the glass and went into the reception area. A clean fresh smell welcomed him as he turned to the right and stood at the reception desk.

The girl behind the glass protective shield was in her early twenties, Fallon guessed, wearing a smart black blazer type jacket, black blouse and he assumed, either black skirt or trousers.

"Good morning, sir. Welcome to the New Mill Hotel. My name is Kirsten. How can I help you today?" Smiled the young lady. Fallon returned the smile.

"I wonder if you can help me." Replied Fallon.

"If I can, sir."

"I'm looking for a friend of mine. A Mr. Robert Foster." Fallon lied.

"Mr. Foster?" Kirsten's face went pale, and her eyes darted from the computer screen to Fallon and back again as if she were trying to figure out what to say next.

"Yes. Robert Foster."

"Are you Mister Whitestone?"

"Yes. Peter Whitestone." Fallon lied for the second time, pulling the first name out of thin air.

"I have an envelope for you, sir. One moment." Fallon turned around and looked around. Three little bays had been formed using two couches and two high backed chairs with a white painted table in the middle of each bay.

A staircase spiralled upwards to the next floor under which was a piano. The smell of freshly made coffee danced with his nostrils.

The area was empty except for a large man with tattooed arms, sitting in one of the high-backed chairs pretending to read a newspaper all the time glancing over towards Fallon, who smiled politely but the gesture was not returned. "Here we go, sir." Fallon, a little startled, turned back around and there was Kirsten pushing the envelope under the small gap at the bottom of the screen. "Sorry about what happened to your friend."

"What?"

"Your friend, Mr. Foster. They fished him out of the river yesterday."

"Ah, yes." Said Fallon pretending to be upset.

"Do the Police have any idea what happened to him?"

"Lead poisoning, I believe." Quipped Fallon. He thanked Kirsten, went towards the exit, and stopped briefly, using the reflection of the exit door to check on tattooed man.

The man had put his paper down and was slowly getting up. Fallon pushed the door opened and went outside. His phone chirped and he pressed '*answer*.'

"K-12." It was Dexter. "We've just received a preliminary death report from the Police. Foster was shot twice at close range. His phone and wallet were missing. Law enforcement are calling it a mugging gone wrong."

"Thanks Dex."

"The colonel wants you back."

"Tell him I am following a lead."

"Can I tell him how long before you're back?"

"Not sure." He pressed '*End Call*' and put his phone away, then did a 180° turn, and headed back towards the hotel, almost knocking tattooed man over. Fallon apologised receiving only a grunt in return.

He stopped and watched as tattooed man crossed the car park and get into a black saloon car, a BMW. Fallon took a mental note of the car; it is number plate and then continued into the Hotel.

Kirsten was still sitting there busy typing in something on the keyboard in front of her. She looked up once she realised someone was standing there.

"Mr. Whitestone. How can I help you?"

"I was wondering if Robert did anything, or went anywhere on the day of his death?"

"He had breakfast up in the restaurant, Mill One, before heading out for a walk on the nature trail."

"Anything else?"

"No. I don't think so."

"Thank you, Kirsten. You've been a great help."

Fallon walked out of the hotel and looked around. The black BMW was still there. Fallon smiled. Then, headed along the side of the second building towards the footpath up to the nature trail, following the same route Foster had, taking pictures on his phone, like any tourist would, occasionally looking back down the trail to see if he were being followed, passing the pipes and the power station, and headed towards the house with the posters in the window.

He stopped outside its front door and bent down to pretend to tie his shoelace. Some movement down the trail caught his attention. Tattooed man, right on schedule.

Fallon smiled again and got up continuing his walk. In his head, he was thinking of where a body would get shot, then tumble into the river, even with help. As he walked, he snapped.

A picture here.

A picture there.

He intentionally slowed his pace so that tattooed man would not lose sight of him, and vice versa. Fallon felt a bit like a spider on a web waiting patiently for an insect, the tattooed man, to get stuck in his webby creation so that he could be disposed of.

Fallon finally came to the fork in the trail where Foster took his fateful decision. He copied and went towards the cliff then quickly ducked out of sight behind a tree, just off the trail, the trap was set. He did not have to wait long, three minutes at most as tattooed man appeared at the edge of the cliff sweating and out of breath, a silenced automatic in his hand. He took out a handkerchief and mopped his sweat ridden brow.

"Mr. Whitestone, where are you?" He wheezed looking around.

"The name's Fallon. Drop the gun!" Ordered Fallon emerging from concealment, the Walther in hand. Tattooed man spun around almost dropping his own weapon. "I said, drop it!" Fallon extended his arms, cupping his P-38 in both hands bringing it up to eye level. He underlined his threat by pulling the hammer back.

"You won't shoot. You're a cop. Cops don't shoot." Grinned Tattooed man, obviously misinformed.

"Who said I was a cop? I didn't... Last chance... Drop the weapon!" The grin disappeared. Fallon could almost hear the tattooed man's thought patterns. "Don't do it!" He warned. Too late. Tattooed man raised his weapon. Fallon fired twice, the classic double tap he had been trained to use. Tattooed man somersaulted backwards as the Walther slugs thudded into him, his automatic spun from his hand, landing several feet away in the mulch.

Fallon shook his head, as he slowly walked across, still covering the man with his weapon. He reached down and felt for a pulse. There was none. "Damn it!" He cursed holstering his weapon and bending down to search the corpse. He found

Foster's phone and wallet but nothing else. No personal identification. He walked over and took out a handkerchief from his pocket and picked up the automatic, putting it in his pocket, wrapped securely in the cloth. He opened his phone and dialled triple nine to report a body. He knew his boss, colonel Scott, was not going to be happy about the way things had worked out.

"What the bloody hell did you think you were doing, K-12?" Bellowed Scott after receiving a talking down from both the home secretary, and the prime minister.

"You were supposed to head to Scotland on a fishing expedition for information, not re-enact the gunfight at the OK Corral!"

Fallon rocked backwards and forwards on his heels trying to endure his superior's rant.

"With all due respect, sir." He began in his defence, "the man came at me first. I was only trying to defend myself."

"Defend yourself? According to the man's autopsy, he has two large holes in his chest big enough for the bloody Titanic to sail back and forth!" Scott dropped into his chair behind his desk. "What were you thinking, man?" Before Fallon could answer, a buzzer sounded, and Scott reached over. "Enter."

Saved by the buzzer, thought Fallon, as Dexter entered. They exchanged brief nods of recognition before Dexter reached for a remote control and pressed one of the numerous buttons.

There was a faint mechanical humming sound before a panel in the wall opposite opened revealing a monitor screen. She pressed another button and up popped tattooed man's face.

"Name. Roberto Rivas. Muscle for hire linked to several killings both here and on the continent. Interpol have a warrant out for his arrest for at least three murders in France alone."

"Seems like I've done them a favour." Commented Fallon. Scott cleared his throat showing his displeasure.

"He's linked to several drug cartels in the States and is also associated with Klaus and Otto Werner." Dexter continued the briefing and pressed another button. Two photos appeared showing two males, twins by the similarities in features. Dark haired in their mid to late thirties. Chiselled features. "I've sent their bios to your phone."

"What about the contents of the envelope K-12 retrieved from the hotel?" Asked Scott.

"It was a locker key, sir. The tech boys believe it's from a bus terminal or train station."

"Do we know where Foster travelled from?" Asked Fallon.

"Golf City."

"Looks like I'm going back to Scotland, sir."

"Yes, quite." Replied his boss reluctantly. Fallon nodded towards Dexter as he made his way to the door and his awaiting Aston. "K-12?"

"Sir?"

"Keep that cannon of yours holstered."

"And I'll make sure my weapon stays concealed too." He smiled. Dexter coughed trying to conceal a laugh. Scott, on the other hand, rolled his eyes and sighed. Dexter followed him out into the outer office where her desk was situated.

She went behind it and pulled open the top right-hand drawer. Reached in, brought out a small envelope, handing it to Fallon.

"Standard travel pass, K-12. Suitable for the train or bus. I recommend the train."

"A plane would be faster." Countered Fallon, hopefully.

"Sorry. Budget cuts." Dexter said with a sarcastic looking smile on her face.

"Are you still pissed at being demoted from a field agent?" He asked.

"What?"

"Never mind!" The door slammed just as her intercom buzzed.

"Sir?"

"Did you give him the travel pass?" Asked Scott.

"Yes sir."

"How did he take it?"

"Badly."

"Well done, Dex. That'll teach him a lesson." A tone of satisfaction resonated from the intercom then it went dead. Dexter smiled a contented smile as well.

11 – *Golf City*

The train journey North took several hours. What Dexter had failed to mention, whether by mistake or intentionally, was that the travel pass only allowed for the basic style of travel, namely, sitting on your ass in a seat watching the world flash by at an incredibly fast speed.

Fallon tried to sleep. Nodding off several times but awoke with a stiff neck. He cursed Dexter. Was this her taking her revenge on her demotion? He made a mental note to discuss this with her when he returned.

Eventually, after a couple of changes at various stations, Fallon got off his train at a substation, linked to the local airbase, which had recently been taken over by the army. He walked off the platform, taking a bridge over the tracks and down the other side. He fumbled in his coat pocket and looked at his train ticket. The number on the stub read 'FB06 OSP'.

There was a small car park next to the train station filled with about a dozen cars, parked neatly in three rows, with about fifteen or so more empty spaces. He walked past all the cars until he found one with the number plate 'FB06 OSP'. His eyes almost popped out when he saw what the registration plate was attached to – a nineteen sixty-nine Ford Mustang.

"A nice piece of kit, isn't she, K-12?" Commented a familiar voice from behind him. Fallon turned to see Cuthbertson standing there.

"She's beautiful."

"Zero to sixty in six seconds thanks to the V8 engine under the hood. Top speed of 128 miles per hour." Fallon's eyes were like saucers as the equipment officer continued his briefing. "Orders from the colonel, you are to respect all the driving laws and try not to damage the equipment."

He tossed the keys to Fallon. The keys fitted snuggly in the door lock and turned smoothly. He opened the driver's door and climbed into the bucket seats.

The Mustang was a two-seater sports coupe with a four-speed gearbox. Fallon put the key in the ignition and turned it on. Its growl was music to his ears. He was still tired from his journey, but the fatigue seemed to wash away at the overture made by this masterpiece of machinery. He closed the door and wound down the window.

"I promise I will take extra care of her, Sparks." He spoke. The equipment officer's response was drowned out by a screech of tyres and the roar of the engine, as Fallon left the car park.

A ten-minute journey, seeing all the rules as asked, brought Fallon to the outskirts of Golf City. According to the tourist blurb he had read on the train, the city was founded in 1413 and is ten miles (sixteen kilometres) southeast from Dundee and thirty miles (fifty kilometres) northeast from the Scottish capital, Edinburgh.

As he drove into the town, he noticed several brightly clothed people playing golf on the courses to his left. On his right were student accommodations and university buildings.

The famous Golf City Hotel passed him on his left now, hiding behind a sports field used by the local secondary school. It may have become famous because of a sport but it was the University that had become its life blood, much to the annoyance of most of the residence.

The population of the city was around seventeen and a half thousand, added to this was around ten and a half thousand students comprising of 145 nationalities, with forty five percent of the countries being from outside the United Kingdom.

An eighth of the student population were from the European Union and a final third from overseas – fifteen percent of those were from the United States. The city is also a renowned tourist destination too. Most of the shops catering for the annual migration of tourist willing to spend their hard-earned bucks on shortbread and tat.

The mustang lazily pulled round a roundabout and took the road up to the right following the signs to the bus station. He found it on the right at the top of the hill and signalled right to enter but had to wait until a large bus pulled out first. He parked his car down the bottom of a hill and walked up. The station was a busy place. All types of people going about their business and their lives. Buses coming and going.

The odd horn honked informing people to watch out as a vehicle was either reversing out to start the next leg of its journey or was coming in to off load its cargo. A couple of men wearing yellow high visibility jackets directed traffic and spoke on radios or to the drivers.

Fallon quickly walked across the concourse and into the main building. The aroma of freshly ground coffee from the snack stands in the corner, mixed with disinfectant, a cleaner was using to mop up some kind of spillage on the floor.

A small boy was sitting on a chair off to the right; crying, while his distraught mother tried to calm him. Fallon walked over to the reception type area where a tall thin man in a pale blue shirt and dark tie, sat behind a glass panel.

"Can I help you, sir?" Asked the man with a broad Scots accent.

"I have this locker key, and I was wondering where your lockers were. I've been asked to pick up something for a friend." Fallon dangled the key in front of the glass, as proof.

"The lockers are off to the right, sir. Just behind the snack bar." Said the man pointing with his finger.

"Thank you." Fallon went to the snack shop and bought himself a coffee, the smell was too hard to resist. Unlike the yuppie set with all their different concoctions, he liked it black with one sugar. He took a sip of the dark tarry liquid before finding and opening the locker.

Inside was a file with the OSP logo on the front, and 'Most Secret' stamped in large red letters diagonally across the front. He unzipped his jacket to halfway and tucked the file inside before zipping it back up.

Locked the locker and handed back the key at the desk. The exit door made a whooshing sound as it opened letting in a cold draft of air that made him shiver slightly. It was then he noticed two men standing across the street both wearing dark sunglasses and staring directly at him. He recognised them from the briefing back at headquarters, the Werner twins.

Fallon turned right out of the door and headed across the concourse. A bus honked at him, but he kept walking, his pace quickening. He took a quick look behind him and saw the twins beginning to give chase. He cursed under his breath as he made it to the top of the road, leading to the car park, and his car.

He started to run. He checked. The twins were also running. Down the road, took a sharp left, nearly knocking an old woman down in the process. He apologised as he quickly checked to see if she was all right. She was a little shaken but otherwise unharmed. He tapped her on the arm and sprinted to his car.

The old woman shouted some obscenities in his direction waving a clenched fist but then ducked for cover as the twins opened fire. Bullets whizzed in Fallon's direction, luckily for him, missing by a mile. He hurried with the car door, eventually opening it, and climbed in.

Started the engine and floored the accelerator pedal allowing the momentum from the car to close the door. Three bullets thudded into the car's body work, and another hit the windscreen.

Another hit, the rear window shattered, as the Mustang roared away out into the traffic. The twins threw their arms up in desperation before putting their weapons away and casually walking back up the hill to their waiting car. Reaching it just as a police car came haring around the corner with headlights ablaze, sirens on and blue lights blinking. It screeched to a halt outside the main building and two uniformed officers almost fell out of the car.

The twins calmly got into their car and drove off in the same direction as Fallon. They hoped to pick up his trail sooner rather than later. Fallon, about ten minutes ahead of the twins, slowed down and looked in his rear-view mirror. Nothing but normal traffic. His breathing slowed too, and he wiped beads of sweat from his brow with the sleeve of his jacket. He decided to travel outside the town, find a secluded spot, and regroup.

He found the spot, a farm track about five miles outside the town and he turned up it, eventually hiding the car at the side of a broken-down barn. Turned the engine off and opened the car door, got out and walked a few paces. *What the hell was Foster and Fuller involved in?* He thought. That is twice he has either been shot at or had a gun pointed at him. This mission was supposed to be a simple missing person. He took out his phone and dialled a secure number. Dexter picked up.

"Fallon?"

"Yes."

"Did you get it?"

"Yeah, but the Werner twins were waiting for me."

"Are you okay?" She sounded genuinely concerned.

"Yeah, but the Mustang took a couple of hits."

"Sparks isn't going to like that."

"Tell me about it."

"What was in the locker?"

"Another file. And before you ask, no. I haven't had time to look at it. I was spending too much time trying not to get my head blown off!"

"Someone's kinda touchy."

"So would you be if...." He began but stop because he realised, he was fighting a losing battle.

"I've taken the liberty to book you into the Park View hotel. I'll send you the directions."

"Thanks, Dex."

"You're welcome, Jake." He was about to hang up when," Jake?"

"Yeah?"

"Stay safe."

"That's my mission in life." Fallon said, trying to reassure Dexter.

Dexter hung up and then realised she was not alone in the office. A woman stood in front of her wearing a white lab coat. She was in her twenties with shoulder length brown curly hair and large circular spectacles.

Small in stature, only five foot two, but what she lacked in height, she made up with both enthusiasm and dedication. She handed a file over to Dexter and left. The name on her identification badge was Elizabeth Klein. Dexter thought for a moment, wondering how long Klein had been standing there and how much she had heard, then dismissed it, opening a file in front of her.

Fallon could hear the worry in her voice. Besides, she rarely called him by his first name. It was either his designation, K-12, or simply Fallon. He hung up and turned to look at the Mustang. The few hits he had mentioned to Dexter were an understatement. The rear window was a hole framed by shards of broken glass. Four bullet holes formed a perfect straight line along the right rear and one of his front headlights was no more.

Deciding it would attract too much attention if he drove it into town, so he moved it into the barn, shutting the doors. He went online and searched for a local taxi firm, noting the number and then coming offline. He dialled the number and waited. Ten minutes later, a grey Qoros 3 2013 saloon pulled up and Fallon got in the back. The driver smiled at him through the rear-view mirror.

"Where to, sir?" The driver asked.

"The Park View hotel, please."

"Of course, sir. There in a jiffy." Replied the driver. His response made Fallon look over to him as he settled himself back into the seat.

The driver was in his mid-twenties with brown skin and jet-black hair, cut high and tight on the sides, but allowed to flow free on top. The man's beard, like his hair, was jet black and clipped tight to his jaw line.

When the driver spoke, and I hasten to add, that Fallon wasn't racist in his remarks, but the driver bobbed his head from side to side, giving him a stupid, almost stereotypical smile, as if the instructions were entering his head, but not lingering around,exiting through the nearest orifice, namely the other ear.

This made Fallon wonder whether this was merely an act, something put on for the tourists, or this man was actually all there in the head.

Fallon sat back and took the opportunity to open the file. It was a mass of papers and photographs showing a couple of different locations in and around Glasgow. The papers turned out to be travel itineraries for several high-ranking officials from different nationalities. One picture in particular caught his attention, the Robyn Smith Centre.

The reason that it stood out, was that it was circled in red marker pen with an 'X' on the main conference centre, and a date scribbled in the corner in biro, the fourteenth, four days away. The Qoros made a right, and then a left, before pulling up in front of what looked like someone's house. Fallon tucked the contents of the folder back in the file and replaced it in his jacket.

"The Park View hotel, sir." Announced the driver. "Here in a jiffy, as promised." Fallon pulled the door handle, opened the car door, before reaching over and handing the man a small bundle of notes.

The driver flicked through the money and his eyes lit up as he realised that the amount was almost triple the fare.

"Keep it." Fallon insisted as he got out.

"Thank you, sir." Fallon started to walk up the three stairs that led to the front door of the house. A sign in the window advertised it as a hotel with three stars. Impressive. The taxi drove off to the end of the street, turned left before stopping.

The driver picked up his mobile and dialled a number. It rang three times before a man picked up.

"He is staying at the Park View Hotel.... Yes...He has the file...I have seen it.... Are you sending someone...... No...You want me to stay and watch...okay.... but it will cost you extra...."

Gone was the stupid smile and head bobbing. His manner was now business like. He hung up and settled down to watch through his rear mirror.

The Park View Hotel was a house that had been converted. Other rooms had been added onto the back of it thanks to an extension. The building itself was a four-storey town house with the three upper storeys being the guest bedrooms. It was run by a mother and daughter partnership, having been handed down through the years on the mother's side.

The entrance hall was quite tight, but the dim lighting made it cosy and welcoming. Upon entering there was a musky smell that greeted Fallon, reminding him of an old Aunt's house he once visited as a child. It had that old person kid of vibe to it, lived in feel.

On the left was the reception desk whilst on the right was the living room / dining room with about half a dozen tables laid out complete with cutlery and napkins. He made his way passed the reception desk and stopped at the stairs.

He looked around for any sign of life. A mixture of polish and some kind on incense stick burning in the background, now toyed with Fallon's senses as he stood waiting. A cough from behind him made him turn around. An old woman with rounded features and brown hair sat behind the desk, she had appeared as if by magic.

"The name's Fallon. Jacob Fallon. I believe you have a room for me." He introduced. The woman put on a pair of halfmoon spectacles and used the point of a pen to scroll down the page of bookings.

"Ah yes. Mr. Fallon. You're in room 007." She reached behind her and unhooked the room key from a wooden board on the wall. "We call it, the Goldeneye Suite." She hissed through her dentures. "Up the stairs, to the third floor, first room on your left. Enjoy your stay."

Fallon started to climb the stairs. The thick carpet seemed to hold on to each foot tread like quicksand. He grabbed on to the banister that snaked upwards on the right. Looked down at the room key, it had the number seven printed on it, not zero-zero-seven. Was this the woman having a joke at his expense or trying to tell him something?

Dexter would have booked the room under some kind of cover story rather than blurting out that he worked for the government. He continued to mull this over as he came to the top of the stairs and turned right. True to what he had been told, there was door number seven. He put the key in the lock and turned it. It clicked smoothly.

He turned the handle and opened the door. There was a window facing him, a small single bed to his right and a chest of drawers with a small television on top to his left. As he entered, he noticed another door on the other side of the bed. He walked over and opened it. The en-suite - a bath, basin, and toilet. Nothing too fancy but functional.

12 – Over in a Jiffy!

He walked over to the window and looked out. A woman was walking her dog and swore when it stopped, squatted, leaving a pile of something brown and smelly on the pavement as it stood back up. The woman looked down at her furry companion, with a look of disgust as she reached into her bag and brought out a small plastic bag, put it around the deposit, picked it up, tying it using the draw strings in the neck.

She looked down disapprovingly at her pooch who looked back at her with big brown eyes, wagging his tail in an attempt to defuse the situation but this just made his owner more annoyed.

She started to walk off and gave a hard sharp tug on the lead to encourage him to follow, which he did. A young couple walked past on the other side of the street, hand in hand, with eyes for nothing but each other. Their conversation, if Fallon hazarded a guess, would be like a babbling brook, making little sense to anyone but the individuals at the centre of it. He kept looking.

Across the road, just within sight, he could see the corner of a powerful looking building. A castle, or what was left of it. The ruins dated back several hundred years, according to the local guidebook, Fallon had found on the table in his room. He decided to give it a visit.

The whole area in front of the ruins, was cordoned off by seven-foot metal railings that some nice person had decided to paint white. As you approached the site, you could not help but notice a path winding down to the beach below. A group of students were down there drinking and having fun.

Entry to the ruins was through the doors of the visitor centre. He pulled one side open and went in. It was just a glorified shop selling all kinds of patriotic tat, from key rings to stuffed toys wearing t-shirts, with the Scottish flag on it.

Fallon went up to the cashier desk and paid for a ticket, following the signs out, into what would have been the courtyard. A group of children were climbing on one of the walls, doing various silly poses, which seemed to please their camera snapping parents.

He walked around, stopping every so often, to read the placards, which had been erected in front of different parts of the castle, each chronicling different moments in history relevant to the area. He saw a sign pointing down a small wooden staircase – the bottle dungeon.

Fallon climbed down the stairs and, there, cut into the hill, was an opening with a metal door and another sign pointing him inside. His interest peaked; he went inside, ducking instantly as the head room almost vanished. He carefully walked down the narrow passageway.

A seaweed smell danced at the back of his throat as he descended deep and deeper. Light came from the electric lights that were bolted to the walls on either side acted like landing lights on a runway, guiding you up and down the passageway.

He heard voices from up ahead of him and managed to get to a wider part of the tunnel, before a small group of Japanese tourists bustled past him, chattering away, and clicking away on their cameras. The tunnel came to a sudden halt at the mouth of a hole in the floor with a ladder leading down. A sign pointed down the ladder promising, 'this way to the mine face.' Well, he had come this far.

Fallon turned around and went down the steps backwards, trying to ignore the sense of claustrophobia, which had suddenly started to overwhelm him.

Instead, concentrating on the task at hand – getting down the metal stairs without catching the back of his head on the rock wall behind him as he descended. He got down the steps safely and turned to face the mine wall. A disappointing sight. It was just a rock face with some small indentations taken out of it.

Fallon imagined paying at the kiosk for one of those guided tours he had seen mentioned in the brochure back at the guest house and he pictured himself following some snotty nosed student as he or she droned on about the history of the place.

Enthusiastically chirping on about the indentations in the wall verbally painting a picture of someone chipping away at the rock to place explosives or something just as ludicrous there, ramping up the excitement with tales of daring do, and using a large amount of artistic licence to boot, for what was probably nothing more than erosion or some asshole taking samples back as a souvenir. Fallon snorted with displeasure.

A shaft of sunlight illuminated part of the face making him look up to where it was coming from – a small ventilation shaft in the roof. Very thoughtful. Feeling slightly underwhelmed, Fallon turned and went back to the ladder. He put his hands on the rails and started to climb.

He looked up just in time to see someone's boot coming down but too late to avoid it as it connected with his jaw sending him crashing to the rock floor below. He landed hard. Lying on his back, dazed from the fall, he was aware of someone climbing down the ladder and coming over to him.

Another smell was added to the seaside aroma he had smelt whilst coming down the tunnel, that of male sweat and bad breath. His attacker was leaning over him now, and something shiny glinted in the artificial light. A blade of some sort. Fallon was in no condition to defend himself, so he braced himself for the blade being inserted.

"Don't worry, old chap. It'll be over in a jiffy." Even in his weakened state, Fallon recognised the voice as that of the taxi driver. His catchphrase was the clincher. His attacker was about to strike when he heard voices, and footsteps on the ladder. He put the knife away and helped Fallon to his feet, just as a family came into view.

"My friend has taken a tumble on the rocks. Be very careful, they're extremely slippery." Advised his attacker.

He propped Fallon against the wall, as the family passed, before climbing back up the ladder and out of sight. Fallon staggered to the ladder and tried to climb, giving chase, but he slumped back, only to be caught by the father of the group, who made him crouch down to get his breath. After a few minutes, and much reassurance, that he was all right, telling the mother of the group that he would get himself looked over at the soonest opportunity.

Fallon slowly made his way to the surface and daylight. There was a small river, a river-ette, dribbling down the middle of the tunnel, which made Fallon's footfall even more treacherous than before. He bumped his head a couple of times on the roof, as his concentration which between placing his feet and minding his head.

Eventually, a shaft of light up ahead told him that he had reached the exit. He came out into bright sunshine, turned left, heading up the stairs and dropped down onto a vacant bench.

He checked the back of his head; a bump was forming and there was some blood. He was going to have a cracking headache shortly.

He sat there for about five minutes but decided to move as he heard the voices of the family echoing from the tunnel. Absence was the best choice he thought as he got to his feet, momentarily steadying himself on the arm rest of the bench before beginning the walk back to the guest house.

What had taken him only a few minutes before seemed to take an age, as he staggered from side to side, colliding with a lamppost and the side wall of a building as he progressed. If you did not know any better, you would have mistakenly thought that he was returning from an all-night bender as some public house. His vision was blurred, and his head was now thumping, as if some internees were trying to escape from inside his cranium.

He got to the front door of the guest house and went inside, managing to get to the stairs before necessity made him grab for the banister to steady himself. His feet clumped heavily up the thick carpeted stairs. He got to the top and paused, breathing and sweating heavily. The person who had attacked him was going to pay but that would have to wait until he had administered some minor first aid on himself.

"Are you alright?" Asked Dexter from the screen of Fallon's phone. He had decided to video call her for an update.

"It hurts like hell, but I'll live." He said holding a bag of ice he had bought from the local shop to the back of his head. "Anything to report?"

"I checked the dates you gave me and there is only one high level meeting happening in Glasgow within the next few days and that something to do with Climate Change. It's been all over the media."

"Yeah. I remember seeing something about it on the news."

"Some of the most powerful world leaders will be there but security will be tight. What do you think they'll try and do?"

"Not sure. Can you do some more digging for me into the Werner twins and see if they have any local contacts."

"I'll see what I can do." She signed off leaving Fallon sitting on his bed nursing the mother of all headaches and mentally vowing to pay the taxi driver back in kind. He looked at his Walther lying on the bed. Pay back is going to be a bitch!

The next day, after popping several painkillers, Fallon was at the bus station, namely at the taxi rank, quizzing the drivers if they knew anything about his attacker in the mine tunnel. Each one shook their heads until he reached the last one, a large man with short grey hair and a grey beard covering multiple chins. As the man spoke, he wheezed.

"Yes, I know him. That's Khalid. Nice young man but only been on the job for a couple of months. I think he lives in town somewhere."

"Thanks. Do you know the address?"

"Hold on a minute, mate. I'll radio my dispatcher and see if he knows." The man reached over to his radio handset onto of the dash and keyed the button. "Oscar-two-nine to dispatch. Mike, are you there?"

"Yes, Steve. What is it?"

"Got a fella here looking for Khalid. Something about an unpaid fare. Any idea where he stays?"

"Wait one." There was silence on the other end, then the sound of a microphone being handled, before, "yeah, one-eighteen South Road."

"Cheers mate. Oscar-two-nine clear." He replaced the handset on his dash and scribbled the address out on the back of a business card before handing it to Fallon. Fallon reached into his wallet, pulled out a twenty and handed it to Geoff.

"Thank you, Steve."

"No, thank you mate."

Fallon used an app on his phone to direct him to South Road and after a few minutes walking up and down, he finally found Khalid's abode. Looking like student flats, or a house that had been subdivided into separate apartments.

Entry was via a buzzer system. He looked down the list of names and found who he was looking for. Because they had already 'met,' Fallon thought it unwise to approach Khalid directly, so he buzzed one of the other numbers.

"Eh...yeah...hello?" Answered a female voice, sounding as if she had just gotten up.

"Yeah, sorry to wake you. I'm the local postie and I have a package for Robert in number three. He doesn't seem to be answering, any chance you can let me in so I can try his door?"

"Whatever!" Replied the female, her voice oozing with a mixture of annoyance and disinterest. A buzzing sound and the door clicked off the latch.

"Thanks." Fallon slowly opened the door. To his immediate right was a plain white door with the tag, 'manager' on it, and a doorbell on the post to the left. A staircase wound its way upwards. He started to climb. After about a dozen or so stairs, they opened out on to a landing.

On the landing were a further two doors, marked one and two. He went up another flight to another landing. Doors three and four. According to the menu on the entrance, Khalid was in flat six. Another landing. Flat five was on the left and six on the right.

Fallon stood outside number six. He reached down and grabbed the door handle and turned it slowly. To his surprise, the door was unlocked. He took out his Walther and pushed the door open, his senses on high alert.

Ears straining. Eyes trying to pierce the gloom looking for any sign of movement. He stopped at a door on his left and put his ear to the wood.

Nothing. He edged further in. The room opened into a bedroom with a double bed. Wardrobe and chest of drawers. A small portable television sat on top of the drawers. There was another door over the other side of the bed. He made his way around and was about to try it went the wardrobe doors burst open, and Khalid launched himself at Fallon.

The two men collided. The impact sent Fallon's gun skidding across the floor coming to a stop under the radiator, which ran the whole length of the window. Both men got to their feet and looked at each other. Both taking up a defensive pose.

"You!" Exclaimed Khalid.

Fallon flashed a brief smile.

Khalid reached into his trouser pocket and took out a flick knife. Fallon took a side on stance where Khalid, being the aggressor, was fuller on. Fallon's hands opened and his elbows bent slightly, as did his knees. Khalid's first lunge was easily parried.

He tried again.

Blocked.

He tried a different tactic and swung the knife in a large, wide arc allowing Fallon to block it again, but also to deliver a punch to Khalid's stomach, making him stagger back a couple of steps.

"Who do you work for?" Asked Fallon.

Khalid charged again. Fallon side stepped, sending Khalid hurdling into the chest of drawers which broke into pieces under the weight, and momentum of the student's collision. The knife dropped onto the floor.

Obscured by some of the rubble from the furniture, Fallon walked over to retrieve his weapon, but Khalid leapt to his feet and jumped onto his back, wrapping an arm around his neck, placing Fallon into a strangle hold. Khalid's other arm was looped under Fallon's left arm and locked up behind his neck.

The two intertwined individuals staggered about the room. They tussled on it for a moment, Khalid eventually gaining the upper hand and getting behind him, his arm curling around Fallon's neck, starting to squeeze the life out of him.

Fallon used his hands to grab onto Khalid's arm, with his fingers on the inside of the arm, near Fallon's chin. He tucked his chin in. Shrugged his shoulders to create a space where he could tuck his chin down to his body and his fingers into the space between Khalid's arm and his chin.

Fallon then tucked his chin into the crook of Khalid's elbow, that is where there is the most wiggle room. Sinking down in this position by bending his knees, which made it more difficult for Khalid to lock his arm onto Fallon's neck. On the side that Khalid was choking him, Fallon stepped his foot back behind Khalid's foot to lock in his leg.

Remembering his training, Fallon didn't arch his back backward. Instead, he kept his back curved forward because if he had arched it the other way, he would render himself defenceless with no balance. He also didn't step out to the side, but back, behind the foot so that his legs were calf-to-calf with his attacker's.

Fallon bent his knees and turned one hundred and eighty degrees towards his stepped foot. His hands still on Khalid's arm, in between Fallon's chin and Khalid's arm.

Once out of the headlock, Fallon pulled diagonally across his body and threw Khalid to the ground. The two men paused for a moment, both trying to regain their composure.

The fight resumed after Khalid caught sight his knife at the same time as Fallon saw his weapon. Both dived. Khalid grabbed his knife and turned only to see Fallon lying on his side pointing the Walther at him. "Who do you work for?" Fallon asked again.

"I can't tell you. He'll kill me."

"And I'll kill you if you don't. Make your choice." Khalid looked first at his knife and then at the barrel of the Walther. Fallon could see him weighing up the odds in his head, odds that were firmly against him.

Fallon decided to even the odds and lowered his weapon, he holstered it, raising his hands to just above hip height, trying to convey that, for now, at any rate, he was not a threat. For a moment, Khalid smiled, and then it disappeared. He had made up his mind. "Don't! I can protect you." Pleaded Fallon.

Khalid shook his head, raised his knife, and charged. Fallon waited till the last possible moment, then side stepped. Khalid shot passed him, the momentum from his attack taking him through the window, only to come crashing to a stop several feet below in a skip.

Fallon made his way slowly to the window and peered over the edge. Khalid's lifeless eyes looked back at him. Fallon surmised that the young man must have broken his neck in the fall. The sound of something beeping as it reversed made him look to his left. The noise was coming from a refuge lorry as it backed up to the skip.

A man jumped out from the passenger side and quickly made his way to the side of the vehicle, secured the sides of the skip onto two metal arms that jutted out from either side of the truck and then pressed a button on the side. Something moaned. The arms lifting the skip complained as they took the weight, lifting it slowly off the ground towards the large gaping hole that led to the insides of the truck.

A couple of shakes and the skip lowered back to earth, emptying its contents in the vehicle. Satisfied, the man secured the arms and jumped back into the truck, which moved off to the next skip.

"Looks like they took out the trash." Mused Fallon before disappearing back into the room. He searched it briefly, knowing that his time would limited because he was almost positive someone from the flats below would either be on their way to investigate the noise made by the fight or be in the phone telling the authorities. His search came up empty, so Fallon cut his losses and left.

"His name was Khalid Masoor." Said Dexter via video link, "according to the university database, he was studying economics and was in his third year. He was a taxi driver in his spare time to get some extra cash. Twenty-one years of age."

"What a waste."

"I'm sure you gave him every chance, Jake."

"That doesn't really help, Dex."

"Sorry. I've done some checking on Masoor and Rivas."

"And?"

"It turns out they were both members of a student organisation called 'Das Wolfsrudel'."

"The wolf pack." Translated Fallon instinctively. Dexter paused, which made him look at the screen. Her face etched with annoyance at the interruption. Fallon smiled a cheeky but apologetic smile. Dexter took this as a sign to continue.

"Going by the group's media posts, they seem pretty extreme, even for a student group. But this is where it gets kinda weird…"

"Oh? How so?"

"The wolf pack is an organization dating back to the nineteen thirties and the era of the Nazi party..."

"And how is that strange?" Asked Fallon, not seeing the point.

"If was disbanded after the fall of the Nazis."

"I see. Well, it looks like someone has taken the time to resurrect it but who? And who would have sufficient power to draw both Masoor and Rivas in? They are from totally different backgrounds. Masoor was a student, and Rivas was nothing more than a thug."

"Money corrupts completely, Jake." Reminded Dexter.

"Any leads on this group?"

"Yeah. It's run by this man..." A picture of a dark-haired man wearing a shirt, tie and blazer popped up. "Meet Viktor Titus."

"Dresses well."

"He should. Comes from money. His father owns a pharmaceutical company in the States called Petirrojo Chemicals. Maximillian Titus."

"Anything on the father to justify his son being involved with this group?"

"Max Titus was born in Germany in the early sixties. Self-made man according to all our sources. Studied in Hamburg before coming to Cambridge to do his honours in chemistry. Set up his first company in the nineties, before going global. Has been very vocal, speaking out against the fake propaganda being circulated about global warming."

"Likes the sound of his own voice, by the sounds of it."

"Possibly."

"He would certainly have the money and the power to fund the Wolf Pack."

"I agree."

"So, what does the disappearance of Fuller, this meeting in Glasgow and the Wolf Pack have in common?" Asked Fallon.

"There must be a link somewhere. I'll keep digging."

"Thanks Dex." He quit the call and went over to his bag and took out the file he had gotten from the locker in the bus station. He opened it, fanning the contents out on the bed so that he could see everything.

13 – 'Bish'

Since taking over as the commander of the Office of Special Projects, James Scott has moved with the times, modernizing departments where needed and also streamlining to cut costs. His main addition was his Intelligence gathering section, or 'I' Section. As the modern world found and started to use the internet, so did the OSP.

Watching and learning as it went. Budgets were allocated for the most up to date equipment and people were headhunted to work said equipment, some from rival agencies or universities, even hackers, were employed to give the OSP the best chance to stay one step ahead of both their rivals and their foes.

Carmella Bishop was the head of 'I' Section. A university graduate and unlike most of the operatives under Scott's command, not military or from a military background. Her whizz-kids or kids, as she affectionately referred to them, constantly watched any chatter over the web or dark web.

Daily reports would be sent to all section heads to keep them appraised of what was happening out in the real world. Bishop hated it when her department was referred to as the I.T. section and they are many documented cases of her almost coming to blows with some of her uneducated colleagues on this very subject.

Bishop is in her late thirties. Slim build with long blonde hair. Her hobbies include keeping fit, martial arts and reading. She lives alone in an apartment in the capital with her cat, Spot. She is a regular feature around the parks and streets around her apartment, especially in the early mornings or late evening, jogging with her earphones in.

It was after one of these early morning sessions, a shower, and a change of clothes, that she went through the usual security checks, and took the lift down to the basement where her section was situated. A retinal and thumb print scanner were the last two obstacles she had to overcome before the door whooshed, allowing her to enter. Her section was laid out like the set of some science fiction television series.

Each of her 'kids' had their own bay, cut off from each other by screens. In each bay, was a comfortable high backed leather gaming chair, a monitor, a desk, and keyboard. Bishop allowed her 'kids' to personalise their own space, with some adding only a few pictures, to others taking it to the extreme with figurines from their favourite television shows or movie franchises. The current choices ranged from Star Wars to the Marvel Universe.

Continuing this relaxed regime, the dress code was extremely casual. Each 'kid' was referred to by their

Christian name, the only exception was Bishop, whom the 'kids' referred to as '*Boss*.' In hushed tones, in the rest rooms, they affectionately called her '*Yoda*' after the all-knowing character from Star Wars. Bishop knew of this other name but kept it to herself, smiling every so often when she saw a bobblehead or figurine of her character on a desk or t-shirt.

Another door whooshed as Bishop entered her own office. Glass on all sides, surrounded by her 'kids.' Like a mummy spider staying connected with her spiderlings through the invisible tendrils of her own private web system. The glass could be tinted or even blacked out at the flick of a switch. She could, using a different switch, put her office into lockdown so that nothing, not even wifi connected systems could breach it.

The room had a couple of bookcases filled with computer language literature, foreign language publications and procedural files. No pictures. No family. She did not even have a steady boyfriend, and she likes it that way. No commitments and no sticky break-ups.

Simple, like the computer code she uses in her daily life. She had a desk, big and wide with a couple of monitors on it, positioned so that she could see both whilst sitting in her large leather seat. She had two keyboards, one in front of each monitor. Again, positioned for comfort. A phone sat off to the right of the desk with multiple buttons on it, linked to the department heads that sat well above her in their ivory towers.

Once a day, normally at the start, mail was delivered. Now, delivery was two-fold. One, the old-fashioned way, by letter or parcel. Each item had been rigorously screened and searched. The second, in this modern era, was by either email or the more outdated facsimile. Again, the emails were put through security whilst the faxes tended to be internal memorandums from above.

A buzz on her intercom. She reached over and pressed a button. Whoosh went the door and in walked the mail man, Paul West.

"Usual crap, this morning." He said cheekily, as he handed Bishop a pile of letters and a small-padded envelope.

"Nothing special, then?" She asked sounding a little disappointed.

"Only that padded bag. It's addressed to K-Section, but Scott wants you to have first look." Said West turning to leave.

"Intriguing." Whoosh went the door and Bishop was alone again. She put the pile of letters to one side and laid the packet down in front of her. She turned it around, over, and back again. A standard padded envelope with bubble wrap layered in the fabric of the envelope, to protect valuable items during transit. She looked at the address label.

FOA COLONEL JAMES SCOTT, INTELLIGENCE HOUSE, WHITEHALL, LONDON

The label was written in bold capital letters and there was no postcode. She turned the packet onto its front to examine the back of it. No sender's details. The alarm bells in her head started to ring. She reached over and picked up her handset, pressed a couple of buttons and waited for an answer.

"Security. Forbes speaking."

"Iain, it's Bish."

"Hi Bish. What can a lowly security officer do for the almighty Bishop today?" Forbes mocked.

"You scanned all the incoming mail this morning, didn't you?"

"Yep. Standard O.P. (operating procedure). Why?"

"It's just that I've been handed a packet meant for K-Section and something smells."

"Has it been opened?"

"Yeah."

"Maybe you should buzz colonel Scott and see what's the lowdown."

"He was my next call after you. I just thought I would cross my tees before bothering him."

"No worries, Bish. That packet was cleared by us at zero-six-fifteen this morning, according to the log I've got up in front of me, right now. In fact, it was me that checked it."

"Thanks Iain. Just thought I'd check."

"No worries."

Bishop put the receiver down and picked it up again dialling the number for K-Section. It ran twice before being picked up.

"K-Section. Dexter speaking."

"Hi Dex. It's Bish. Is the colonel in?"

"One moment." The sound of clicking could be heard on the line and then Dexter's voice returned, "I'm afraid he's in a meeting now. Can I help?"

"It's about this package you sent down to me. Any heads-up?"

"Yeah. We received it up here earlier this morning. It came with a note and a thumb drive. As soon as the Boss read the note, he sent it down to you for analysis."

"Okay." Replied Bishop warily.

"The note mentions a group we're currently investigating in an on-going operation, and we would like your insight on it. Background and any extra Intel you can give us would be appreciated."

"I'll see what I can do, Dex." Bishop hung up and sat there looking down at the packet. She eventually plucked up the courage and lifted the package, upending it so that the contents spilled out onto her desk. There were only two items – a piece of typed paper and a thumb drive. She picked up the piece of paper and started to read.

'*Colonel Scott,*

You don't know me, but you worked with my father at the Office of Special Projects. His name was Eric Fuller. I am sorry to inform you that my father passed away a few days ago unexpectedly. I received this thumb drive through the mail a few days later with strict instructions to forward it to you and only you. I hope you can shine some light on how this links in with my father's death and I look forward to hearing from you.

Sincerely

Gregor Fuller'

Bishop re-read the note again trying hard to read between the lines, looking for any hidden coding, or thread she could work with, but she could not find anything. She laid the note down and was about to pick up the drive when her intercom buzzed again, nearly making her jump with fright. Whoosh! And in walked Elizabeth Klein, or Lizzie to her friends, one of Bishop's top analysts.

"You've done it again, Lizzie." Congratulated Bishop.

"Boss?" Said the analyst, lost on why she was receiving praise.

"You read my mind. I was about to buzz for you, and you walked in the door. Spooky."

"That's why you pay me the big bucks, boss." Smiled the analyst.

"I need you to look at this for me and glean everything you can from it." Bishop handed Lizzie the thumb drive.

"Okay boss." Lizzie turned and, was Bishop mistaken, did Klein skip towards the door, wait for it to open, and skip out.

Nah! Surely not. She dismissed it with a shake of her head before placing the note in a vacant folder, placing it in the second drawer of her desk.

Klein returned to her desk, decked out in all things Harry Potter. A mouse mat and a mug included in the things adorning her cubicle. There was even a sign on the back of her chair stating, 'no muggles allowed.' She put the thumb drive into the side of her laptop, picking up a pen from her HP mug and sticking the end in her mouth.

Chewing the end of a pen or pencil helped her think. She had done it since Primary school, much to the annoyance of her teachers, later her professors and tutors at university. Her fingers were a blur as they seemed to glide over the keyboard. Only stopping to push her glasses back on to the bridge of her nose. The same files came up Gregor had found but Klein opened them and downloaded them, giving each their own separate file on her screen.

Three hours later, the door to Bishop's office whooshed open and Klein came almost tumbling through the door. She was so excited, that when she tried to speak at first, the words were nonsense, and she had to take a moment to regain her composure. Bishop offered her a glass of water which she politely refused, taking the remote from the top of her boss' desk and pointing it at the blank screen in the wall, which instantly flickered into life revealing page upon page of data.

"What does the term 'Wolf Pack' mean to you?" Began Klein turning to her boss for an answer.

"If my old history lessons were anything to go by, weren't they the names given to the German U-boats that prowl the Atlantic during the Second World War?"

"Correct, but also wrong." Seeing the puzzled look on Bishop's face, Klein continued, "it was also the name given to a top-secret organisation in Nazi Germany, made up of top industrialist and military officials tasked by Hitler to find a way on continuing the Third Reich after his death. Various attempts were made to engineer super or wonder weapons, super soldiers, designed through cloning.

They even made a run on several of the big banking firms, to finance some of their projects." She turned to look at her boss to see if she was still paying attention. She need not have worried, Bishop sat motionless, like a statue, eyes glued to the screen, ears tuned in to the briefing. "The whole organisation was supposed have collapsed when Hitler committed suicide in the bunker in Berlin and the main perpetrators fled the oncoming Red Army.

Most were caught and either disappeared or were put on trial for war crimes, at Nuremberg, and other such tribunals. However," Klein paused, "it was rumoured back then, in the halls of the Intelligence communities, that not all the high-ranking officials were captured, several allegedly escaping to South America and elsewhere."

An hour later, Klein was continuing this same briefing via video call, in front of all the ranking officers of the OSP, the government and foreign agencies deemed to have an interest.

"Pieter Titus, the father of Industrialist Maximillian, was one of these to have links with '*Das Wolfsrudel*' or the Wolf Pack, though nothing has been proven. I also found a link to an Allied operation codenamed '*Operation Dionysus*,' a member of that team was Major James Fuller, the father of the missing Gregor Fuller, who sent us this."

"I remember reading about Dionysus at OSP training. Wasn't it the Allied attempt to stop the Germans from mass producing some kind of wonder drug that could keep their soldiers fighting with no ill effects." Added Scott.

"Correct, sir." Replied Klein.

"According to my research, ably helped by Miss Dexter, the Allies zeroed in on some factory in Greece. The Germans were using an old vineyard and winery to hide the underground factory they had built to produce the drug."

"Did they ever get around to making any?" It was the British Home Secretary, Lady Amy Spence.

"Not according to allied intel, madam secretary. The commando unit that hit the factory, led by Fuller, blew it to kingdom come and back again. The explosion could be seen several miles away, and even from the submarine, waiting to take the raiders off."

"How did Titus escape prosecution?" asked vice admiral Walker, joint chiefs.

"Maybe I can help with that." Replied Darla Hayes, director of the Central Intelligence Agency. She had taken over the intelligence mantel from her grandmother, after whom she was named. "After the war had ended, the Allies, especially the United States, helped certain individuals escape justice depending upon their value."

"Wasn't it called 'Operation Paperclip' or an off shoot of it?" Asked Dexter, her knowledge of history rising to the surface, once more, bringing a pleased smile from Scott. Hayes nodded uncomfortably.

"Yes Miss Dexter."

"And by value, you mean how they could help your country get a foot up on the Russians." Suggested Scott.

"Yes colonel. You could put it that way. It was a different era, back then."

"Anyway, Titus was a well-known chemist, and we moved him to the States, setting him up in Oregon, giving him enough money to start up, under the supervision of the CIA, of course."

"And now, some seventy plus years later, it had come back and bitten you in the ass!" Added Monsieur Pierre Gallon, French Ambassador to the United Kingdom, who rarely minced his words. An argument ensued with each invitee trying to talk over the others. It was a cacophony of sound only stopped by a loud ear piecing whistle from Bishop.

"Thank you, Bishop." Thanked Hayes before she dropped a bombshell. "According to our records, and these have been triple checked you Brits, in the Office of Special Projects, assisted Titus in escaping in Forty-Six." The room went quiet. You could hear a whole box of pins drop, as those present tried to digest Hayes' accusation.

"Where's your proof Hayes?" Demanded Scott. On cue, an official looking, dated, memo popped up on the screen. It was on official OSP headed paper and 'MOST SECRET' stamped right across it in bold red ink. It instructed the operatives in Germany to get Titus and his family to a rendezvous codename '*Point Zulu.*' It went on to say that they would be airlifted out to an undisclosed destination.

"Look at the signature at the bottom." Invited Hayes, smiling like the cat that had nicked the cream. Each invitee leaned forward towards their screens for a closer look. Scott and Bishop's chins hit the floor in utter shock.

COLONEL J. FORRESTER

Again, the room was silent in disbelief. Bishop looked up at Scott and then at Klein. No words. Just shock etched on their faces. The home secretary broke the silence.

"You said this has been verified director Hayes?"

"Yes, madam secretary."

"Then we should have a copy in the archives. I will get back to you." Her screen went blank.

14 – *Phoenix*

A few days later, Amy Spence had gotten back to Scott and confirmed that she had found collaborating evidence buried deep in the archives at the Imperial War Museum in London. This sent shockwaves through all the departments that were privileged to know. The core beliefs and standards laid down in stone by the first director of the OSP were blown away in an instant, like ash from a campfire. Play the espionage game but always return home. Well, they had played and lost.

Meanwhile, somewhere on the mainland, a computer beeped. Igor Marinko, who had just finished a video conference call with his superiors, spun round in his chair and looked at the screen. A warning message had appeared informing him that someone was, or had been, looking at a file that had been dormant for several years, if not decades. The file was entitled '*Operation Dionysus*.' He reached over and picked up the phone, dialled an internal number and spoke for a few minutes to the person on the other end in Russian before hanging up.

He sat there staring at the screen, drumming his fingers, as was his ritual when deep in thought. A knock came at his office door before a man dressed in an Army Captain's uniform entered, walked forward, and saluted before handing him a manila folder, did a sharp 180 degree turn then left.

Marinko opened the folder and started to familiarise himself with the operation.

After about thirty minutes, he closed the folder and took off his spectacles before rubbing his tired eyes. He let out an exasperated breath before picking up the telephone again and dialling another number, this time several digits long. The line on the other end chirped five times before a male voice answered in Russian. A few pleasantries were exchanged before Marinko pressed a red button at the side of the keypad securing the line.

"Colonel Macheyov, why, after all these years, would the CIA and the OSP be looking into 'Operation Dionysus'?" Asked Marinko.

"No idea, comrade Marinko. That operation died seven decades ago along with most of the people involved."

"Don't you think it a little curious that they are looking into this a few days before the summit in Glasgow?"

"Very curious but what has a seventy-year-old wartime operation got to do with a modern-day summit on climate change?"

"Do we still have operatives in the area?" Asked Marinko. There was a momentary silence on the other end as the head of the Federal Security Service, the FSB, mulled over his reply.

"That is classified, comrade. Above your paygrade, as the Americans would say. However, I will investigate it. The Motherland thanks you for your diligence, comrade Marinko." Before Marinko could reply, the line went dead. He slammed the phone down and was left staring at the file in front of him.

In Moscow, however, Macheyov was far from sitting still. He was straight on the internal line to his superior, the president. The line rang once before the familiar tones of Iryna Popov answered, the president's personal secretary.

Macheyov explained that he needed to speak to the President urgently on a most pressing matter, but was flobbed off by Popov, saying that the president was in a meeting and left instructions not to be disturbed.

It was Macheyov's turn to slammed down the phone, swearing aloud. He sat for a moment staring ahead, his chin resting on his fingertips. His mind whirring like an outdated computer as it tried to digest the information.

Suddenly, he slammed his hands on his desk and reached over for his phone once more, dialling a long number and waited. It chirped. He waited. It chirped. Still waiting. It chirped several times, and he was about to hang up when a female voice answered.

"Yes."

"The phoenix has died." Macheyov said cryptically.

"But it will arise anew from the ashes." Came the response.

"Do they know?"

"No."

"Are you secure?"

"Yes."

"Your office has been nosey."

"I know."

"Who has been assigned?"

"K-12."

"Do we know him?"

"Fallon. Jacob Fallon."

"Fallon? That name sounds familiar."

"Great-grandson of Jonathan Fallon."

"Ah yes. Forrester's little lap dog."

"My instructions?"

"If he gets too close, kill him. Do you have a problem with that?" Macheyov said coldly.

"No."

Macheyov hung up and rested his chin on his fingers again but unlike the earlier time, a small pencil thin smile came across his face. In his spare time, he liked to play the game of chess. He was not a master of the game by any standards, but liked the tactics involved of trying to out-think your opponent.

Trying to stay several moves ahead which was not unlike the human game of chess he was currently involved in. In those terms, this would be the opening gambit. How would his opponents in the Office of Special Projects respond? Defence or attack.

Marinko had now left his office and got into his official diplomatic transport, a Mercedes E-Class with modifications. He had personally picked this model for its reliability and comfort. He sat in the back as his driver and FSB bodyguard, Yuri, drove them through the afternoon traffic on the way to his town house.

"You look tense sir. If you don't mind me saying so." Commented Yuri.

"I have a lot to think about, my friend. Please, isolate me." Yuri nodded and pressed a button on his dashboard. A soundproof pane of glass silently moved up and hissed into place, separating driver from passenger, allowing Marinko to conduct business without Yuri eavesdropping.

He took his mobile out of his pocket and dialled a number which was answered instantly by a woman's voice.

"Did he phone?"

"Yes. Like you said he would."

"And?"

"He wants me to keep an eye on the investigation into Dionysus."

"And?"

"If they get too close, I am to eliminate the lead operative."

"Who is the lead?"

"Fallon." Marinko swore. "Do you know him?"

"Our paths have crossed several times over the years. He is like a bulldog who will not let go."

"That is unfortunate." The female voice said emotionless.

"Very. Does he know that you are working for me?"

"No."

"Good."

"What are my orders?"

"Carry out your mission as instructed unless you hear from me."

"Understood."

"Phoenix?"

"Yes?"

"Be careful."

"As Fallon once said, That's my mission in life."

Marinko smiled as he hung up. His mind drifted back to the file he had read in his office. It highlighted what the Americans had done during the closing months of the war, but it also told a story of deception and intrigue on the part of Mother Russia too. Both superpowers were just as guilty as the other although none would admit it in public.

His black Mercedes glided to a halt outside his white stoned town house. Yuri skirted around the side and opened the rear passenger door, allowing Marinko to climb out. It had started to snow. He looked up at the heavens, pulling the collar of his jacket around his neck, thanked Yuri, saying, he would not be needing him for the rest of the evening, before heading up the stairs and went inside closing the door behind him.

His return was monitored by the security camera perched high up in the corner of the roof, just to the left of the door. It looked down on the front door but could pan up and down slightly to encompass part of the street leading up to the house.

A grey suited security guard sat in a small office, at the back of the building, wrote down on a pad the time and date of Marinko's arrival, before picking up a telephone, dialling a number and reporting that Marinko had returned safely. The security guard yawned and stretched.

He took off his jacket and draped it over his chair revealing his shoulder holster and the butt of a Izhmech PSM automatic pistol. He settled down, to watch the four screens in front of him, as he unscrewed his thermos flask and poured some of the steaming liquid into a mug that had the Russian flag on it.

Not the stripy disgrace of the Federation but the red one with the gold hammer and sickle on it. He was a proud Russian but a supporter of the old ways, not the new, and he was not scared to show it.

News had filtered through to Fallon via Dexter. She gave him the briefest of updates. Although Fallon was stunned by the news that his hero, Forrester, had been implicated in smuggling known Nazis out of Germany, he could see on Dexter's face that she was taking it hard.

Most of the younger operatives grew up on stories of Forrester's daring adventures, as if he were some kind of hero, from one of those trashy pulp magazines. The escapade in Egypt in 1916, when Fallon's great-grandfather had been recruited to the OSP and together with help from a small band of soldiers, stopped a German attempt to change the course of the war. Fallon had a personal stake in the Forrester legend.

Backlash from the 1916 operation, was that Fallon's great-grandmother and his grandfather, were kidnapped and held for ransom, forcing his great-grandfather to come out of semi-retirement, to save them. And now this hero image that had been carefully crafted by the spin-doctors was about to go pop like an over inflated children's party balloon.

He signed off with Dexter and sat there on his bed trying to understand where this left '*Operation Shattered Truth.*' To clear his head, he decided to head to the beach. Fallon grabbed his jacket and headed out.

The walk to the beach took seconds. A turn right from the Hotel and then a left and you were on the coastal path, or that is what the blue and white tourist sign advertised it as. He pulled the collar of his jacket up and hunched his shoulders as he leaned into the wind that had suddenly picked up. Other people had decided to brave the evening. A couple of dogwalkers chatted as their pooches smelt each other's butts.

A group of school kids from the local secondary school laughed and pointed at the canine's antics. Another group, of about seven or eight, students this time, jostled and barged their way along the path not caring who they bumped into or annoyed. Fallon took avoiding action as one of the females collided with him. A pretty brunette with little between the ears, as she just giggled, and said something that resembled an apology.

They continued their merry way shouting and swearing. The shouting was utterly pointless because each part of the whole, was only a matter of a couple of feet away, at any one time, but hey-ho, which is students for you. Fallon came to the top of the hill. To his right was the ruins of some kind of ancient hospital that a group of East Asian tourist were taking great delight in snapping each other standing on. He looked down at the vista that opened in front of him. To his left, was the harbour and a small family run café.

To his right, were posh looking flats and a road that split into two – with one continuing along the boat marina and the other going sharp right up past a private school and heading off back into town.

There was a small metal bridge that spanned the harbour under which sluice gates kept back the sea water, allowing enough to keep the several boats and yachts bobbing at anchor. The smell of the seaside played with his nostrils.

The mixture of seaweed and rotting sea-life. It took him back to his childhood when he used to go to the seaside with his mother on daytrips. Ride the donkeys, eat the chips out of newspaper, or lick an ice-cream. He walked down the steps that were overgrown with weeds and went passed the café. The smell of chips made his stomach complain. His feet clanked across the bridge and then it was up and round back onto the path.

Now, to his left was the beach, open to the elements. To his right was a large piece of grass that used to be a putting green, before the council budget cuts, or at least, that is what one of the leaflets on the desk in his room said.

Seagulls screeched and circled overhead plucking up the courage to dive bomb unsuspecting tourists, as they munched on their chips. Several black dots bobbed up and down in the water. Fallon found it hard to distinguish between swimmers and seals.

A brave soul braved the elements on a paddle board while those less adventurous ran for cover as the rain started to get heavier. His pace quickened. Along past the sailing club, the Maritime Study Hub loomed large, on his right, new building that the designers had tried to age and failed, down a small hill and back up.

To his right, like some huge earth monster, the swimming pool burst forth. He went down a couple of stairs and round to the front of the building. It was named after the beach that sprawled out in front of it.

A sign warned users of the car park, that it closed early at weekends, and their modes of transport ran the risk of being locked in until the following day. He turned to go into the building, but the door did not budge. He moved to the one on his right and it hissed open allowing him into the inner sanctum, a small atrium with a notice board on the wall advertising memberships and the pool programme, a couple of large plastic recycling bins sat, to his right, with mouths open, like the gulls he had just left outside, waiting to be fed.

The glass on the windows could do with a clean, he thought as he went through the inner door.

A typical swimming pool smell welcomed him, a mixture of bleach and sweat. He paused and looked around. A small shop on his left sold what you would expect – swimwear, floats, and goggles.

The main reception desk was on his right. It had two positions, both occupied, one with a large grey-haired woman with a face that would melt the hardest metal and the other had a woman in her early fifties with blonde hair tied in a ponytail and wearing glasses. In front of him was a staircase that, led to the second floor. Various signs hung from wires directing you to different parts of the building.

The blonde was deep in conversation with a mother trying to pay for some kind of lesson, but the older woman was free. Fallon walked over and greeted her with a warm smile.

"Can I help you?" She asked with a tone that made Fallon feel as though he was interrupting her from doing something else.

"Yes, is there any place I can go and get a coffee?"

"We don't have a café anymore. It will have to be from a vending machine." She said tersely.

"That's fine."

"Under the stairs and through the double doors." She pointed a bony witch like finger in the general direction. Fallon followed her directions and pushed one of the doors open. Now, to his right were two glass backed squash courts. The aroma of sweat intensified.

Groans, grunts, and swearing emanated from each court as two pairs of male individuals competed to better their opponents at hitting a small black sphere as hard as they could against the walls. He ignored the gladiatorial contests and searched out the correct machine, putting his money in and pressing a button for milky coffee.

There was a pause before a brown plastic cup dropped down and a whirring sound as it was filled with hot liquid. He waited until the machine had stopped before picking up the cup.

Fallon decided to have a look around and followed the sign to the poolside viewing gallery, turning left and then along a small narrow corridor before opening a heavy wooden door, taking him out onto a seated area next to the pool. A light in the roof, high above flickered on and off and the noise seemed to rise as he sat down on one of the plastic chairs which seemed to come in three distinctive colours – orange, yellow and grey.

His was orange. Several homemade laminated signs in front of him expressly forbade him from using his mobile in this area. He assumed that it had something to do with child protection only for his assumption to be proven when one of the lifeguards came across and explained to a pompous looking older woman that she was not allowed to use her mobile.

The woman did not take being told off very well and continued to berate both the rule and the person telling her. For his sake, the lifeguard walked away leaving her talking to herself. Fallon sat there silently listening to her. She had no leg to stand on but must enjoy hearing herself.

A large sign on the wall off to his right advertised the Trust running the building with its web address underneath. Light came from three sources, the artificial ones in the roof, large windows that surrounded the pool on three sides and a large sky light shaped like a pyramid in the middle of the roof. There were two pools – a toddler's pool with parents and babies bobbing about and a main pool.

The main one was your typical leisure pool. Twenty-five metres long and eight metres across. There was a lane rope in, so that those that wished to, could swim lengths uninhibited by children or families getting in their way. A large flume snaked its way back in on itself ending in a splash pool. Large planet-like balls hung from the roof.

Decoration or noise reducing or both. Three lifeguards stood on duty. One off to his left, at the shallow end, which had just been in conflict with the woman who was still speaking to herself, one at the entrance to the flume, which was at the top of a winding staircase, and one sitting on a chair elevated six feet from the floor looking down godlike on the swimmers.

The odd whistle from the lifeguards, accompanied by either a point, or a shake of the head. Fallon sat back and crossed one leg over the other, sipping the hot liquid, realising how plasticky it tasted, making him remember why he never drank the office coffee. He noticed that the lifeguards ranged in ages – ones that looked as if they had just come out of nappies, to those at the end of their careers, in their fifties or even sixties. One of the older lifeguards was trying to instruct a child of about nine to dive.

The lifeguard seemed to be in his element, distracted by the child's feeble attempts to enter the water in a straight, or streamlined, position, whilst the father, a few metres away, held onto the side of the pool and applauded his offspring's attempts, which mostly ended in a fabled belly flop, which added fuel to the lifeguard's coaching session.

A practice that Fallon thought highly dodgy considering, he thought, the lifeguard was supposed to be watching the pool. No one, however, looked like they either noticed or cared. Fallon looked down at the other end of the pool, at the other lifeguard and saw a look of frustration on the man's face.

He was obviously pissed off with what his colleague was doing at the other end, as the odd shake of his head demonstrated. However, this lifeguard was a professional. His demeanour signified that as he prowled the shallow end of the pool, like a cage wild beast, his head slowly moving from side to side, his hands clasped behind his back.

He would stop periodically and simply watch or walked briskly across to the smaller circular shaped pool where younger children bobbed about like corks whilst their parents chatted to one another, to tell an older child for coming down the dolphin shaped slid headfirst. One of the chatty parents would stop talking and look over to see what was going on.

A question would be asked and answered. Then, the lifeguard would return to patrolling leaving the parent to chastise the child long after the event had happened, closing the barn door after the horse had bolted.

Fallon sat there for another ten minutes taking in his surroundings. A young woman in her twenties came from the showers. This was nothing unusual except she was wearing very little in terms of swimming attire. A simple piece of material covering her breasts and a pair of briefs that were trying to escape between her butt cheeks.

Anal flossing, now there is a thought that Fallon would find hard to purge from his consciousness for a while. He watches her saunter across to the edge of the shallow end and dip her toe in the cool water. Her long blonde hair cascading over her shoulders like a lion's mane. Her head moving, first towards the right-hand side of the pool and then to the left as if she were trying to decide which side to go into.

The pool had been portioned off – on the left was a swimming lane which was one and a half the size of a normal lane, which equates to about three metres.

The right-hand side was the rest of the pool, five metres in width, and set aside for public swimming. It was then, the lifeguard at the shallow end passed her. She asked him a question and the guard, using both verbal and hand gestures answered her. Going by the look on her face, the response didn't sit well with her plans.

The lifeguard said something else and then continued his patrol. It was then, Fallon noticed that the young woman was carrying a net bag with what he assumed was her name scrawled on it in permanent marker. She dropped this down at her feet and slipped into the swimming lane, glancing briefly at the plastic sign propped up at the mouth of it, telling swimmers to swim clockwise, whilst using arrows to enforce the direction to be swum.

She reached over and pulled her swim bag towards her, pulling open the mouth like a dentist about to perform a dental examination, and pulling out her equipment. A swimming cap and a pair of swim goggles. She placed them on the side and then coiled up her hair, picked up the cap and put her chin to her chest before pulling the plastic over her head, turning it into a large orange zit.

She tucked any stray strands of hair underneath and then put her goggles on her head, leaving them just above her painted eyebrows.

She delved once more into her sack, like a female Santa Claus about to hand out a wrapped present to some snotty nose little turd that was sitting on her lap and pulled out a set of dark blue swim fins, the type divers use, and a set of lime green hand paddles. A voice from above made her look up.

It was the lifeguard. Another verbal exchange. Another version of her plan shattered as she shoved the paddles and fins back in her bag.

She raised her hands up in despair, but the guard was having none of it. He spoke to her and, explained the reasoning behind his ruling. She shook her head in disbelief, turned and pushed off, breaking into quite a decent freestyle.

She swum up and back, fifty metres and then stopped, reached back into her bag and pulled out a piece of paper, read it for a moment, and then pushed off again, this time, her arms being thrown forwards together and a two beat dolphin kick under the surface propelling her forward as she launched herself up the lane doing butterfly.

Fallon looked across at her nemesis, the lifeguard, who turn it was to throw his arms up in despair. He shook his head and walked slowly across and waited for the swimmer to return. She came into the wall fast, preparing to do a tumble turn but the guard, showing his experience, was ready for her, as he tapped her gently on the soles of her feet with a spare float. She stopped and looked up at him angerly.

Another exchange. This time, the guard pointed to the sign that, moments before, she had pretended to digest, and a verbal tennis match ensued, both participants becoming more animated as the conversation progressed, making Fallon wish he were a trifle closer so that he could listen in.

The lifeguard reached for his radio that was clipped to his hip. Fallon was not sure whether he intended to use it or not, but the gesture was sufficient for the swimmer to concede defeat. She swam off once more and the guard returned to his patrol.

Moments later, two male lifeguards appeared through the door to Fallon's left, the lead one unhooking a rope that was across the gap between the barriers. They both took the two steps onto the poolside with care, noticing a pool of water left by a swimmer.

The duo walked across to the guard at the shallow end, had a brief discussion, which cause their colleague to look at them in disbelief, shake his head and then walk up the side of the pool towards the deep end.

Fallon was about to leave but the reaction from the guard perked his curiosity, and he decided to stay and see what developed. One of the newcomers was kneeing down on the poolside screwing in a bolt which fastened a bracket with a hoop on the end to the side of the pool. Twenty-five metres away, at the other end, two of his colleagues were pulling out a lane rope from a large drum, one pulling and the other turning a large wheel that closely resembled the steering wheel of a ship.

The rope was pulled along the side of the pool, the guard doing the demanding work was attached the lane rope via a bright yellow piece of rope hooped around the hook at the end. It looked like a major logistics operation was being enacted in front of Fallon's eyes and he marvelled at the ease the staff dealt with it.

Two lifeguards remained vigilant, watching the water, whilst another two pulled the lane rope into the water, the guard at the deep end getting the harsher deal as he had to pull it over a pair of starting blocks that rose out of the pool floor like zombies from their graves, each permanently bolted to the floor.

Up and over. Up and over. Then down on to one knee, a glance to the other end to see if it was secure and then the cranking began, the lane rope, once limper than a wet paper bag soon became straight and tight.

The student who had been causing the grief smiled with delight, but this was soon dashed by one of the other guards, who walked across and asked her to move to the other half of the pool.

She looked at him in disbelief, another brief conversation, the guard reached for the radio clipped to his hip, another verbal tennis match and then the student gave up, swam front crawl to the shallow end, hopped out, grabbed her stuff and stormed into the showers.

A woman dressed in an official looking t-shirt and dark leggings walked onto the poolside from the showers carrying a clipboard. She was in her early thirties, Fallon's best guess, with a tattooed left arm. Her hair, dark, brown, was pulled back into a ponytail.

Small circular 'Harry Potter' style glasses were perched precariously on the bridge of her nose. Behind her, parade ten swimmers of various ages from what looked like school children to one that looked like an extra from one of those Nordic historical dramas you see on the television, complete with dreadlocks and tattoos. Each nervous. Heads darting from side to side, scoping the arena they were about to do battle in, like gladiators of old.

Fallon overheard one of the lifeguards speaking to a parent a feet metres to his right, telling the interested adult that the people that had just arrived, like Snow White and the Seven Dwarfs, were candidates taking part in a lifeguard training course. She asked if this was their first day, to which the guard replied that it was their third. The adult thanked him and sat back in her chair.

The drama on the poolside over, Fallon deciding that he had warmed up enough and it was time to leave. He got up and went to the exit door which opened as if by magic. He stopped, to allow to young female lifeguards to walk through.

One was slightly smaller than him in height with tanned skinned and long dark hair. The other was of similar height but with brown hair. Each carried a name badge on their chest. The dark-haired one was called Amy, whilst the other was Lauren. Both smiled at him as he waved them through.

15 – *Das Wolfsrudel*

Viktor Titus looked on with pride at the ensemble in front of him. Students like himself that cared about the environment. Young men and women from all walks of life and backgrounds, nationalities, and skin colours. Their clothing matched by their diversity. They waited outside their halls of residence, Ayton House, for the chartered bus that would take them to Glasgow and the conference. Wooden placards either hung at their sides or were propped up against the wall of the building, in anticipation of their journey and their rally.

Some called it a demonstration of people power. Inwardly, Titus called it a way to a means. An opportunity that his group, '*The Wolf Pack*,' could use to further their own agenda. Several of its members were strategically secreted amongst the demonstrators, ready, on his signal, to cause as much disruption as possible as a distraction to the real agenda, the contents of which only he knew.

His father would be proud. Two of the group dressed in multi-coloured clothing humped a large hold-all, on to the picnic table, which sat at the side of the building, flanked by two long wooden benches. There was a sudden bellow from a horn and the bus appeared at the top of the road. It stopped in front of the group and the door opened.

Seeing the hold-all, the driver pressed a button on his dashboard and the side storage bays opened. The hold-all was humped down and then slid underneath. Two other men, the Werner twins, also had an identical hold-all, but they effortlessly put it underneath and Klaus nodded in Viktor's direction.

"What's in the bags mate?" Asked the driver as Viktor climbed aboard.

"The first one is supplies – food and the like. The second is leaflets and propaganda we are going to be handing out at the rally on Glasgow Green." Replied Viktor before making his way up the bus and sitting at the back so that he could watch everyone getting on. He recognised most of those who got on.

Some from the Climate change meetings he had attended, when he originally thought up the plan he was about to embark on, and some who were members of the Pack. Things evolve. That was the philosophy of his father. Nothing stays the same if it wants to survive. The original Wolf Pack ideology was deemed out of date by the turn of the new millennium.

Max Titus began the process whilst using his pharmaceutical company as a front, to gain a foothold with governments, and policy makers around the world.

Who does not want to be linked with a company that helps cure a disease or becomes the next fad.

Think of the public relations coup for those in high office and the financial rewards that come with it. The classic carrot and stick approach. The carrot being the rewards whilst the stick was intelligence on rivals and warning if the authorities started to sniff around a particular product.

Intelligence was power. Max became one of the most powerful men in industry. He knew the right people. Greased the right palms. His network grew like an enormous invisible spider's web with him at the centre.

Now, after over twenty years in the planning, 'Operation Hummingbird' would become a reality just like its namesake did back in the Nineteen Thirties – to purge all nonessential waste, from the top tier of world government, so that a new leader could appear.

In 1934, Nazi Germany, under the rule of Adolf Hitler, ordered a series of political extrajudicial executions, intended to consolidate his power, and alleviate the concerns of the German military about the role of Ernst Rohm and the Sturmabteilung (SA), the Nazis' paramilitary organisation, known as 'Brownshirts.'

Nazi propaganda presented the murders as a preventive measure against an alleged imminent coup by the SA under Rohm – the so-called Rohm Putsch. It began on June 30th and finished on July 2nd. 'Operation Hummingbird' was also known as 'The Night of the Long Knives.'

Titus would plant a bomb during a summit of some kind and blame it on the far-right group called 'Das Wolfsrudel.' He had ordered his tech geniuses to post anti-government rants and threats, on all the social media platforms, even using his dim-witted son, to front some of them. But he needed a global meeting to achieve his aim, then along came the Climate Change summit in Glasgow, like a moth to a flame.

Of course, security would be off the chart because of the number of dignitaries that would be attending. Hell, there was even a rumour circulating that a famous movie star would be making an appearance, icing on the cake as far as Titus was concerned. There would also be the usual groups protesting about the meeting and groups protesting about those groups and so the cycle continued.

His son was the ideal patsy. Brought up in a carefully constructed world of capitalism, gone rampant, but then from an early age, have his ideals turned against such things, by carefully placed individuals, that his father employed for that very purpose. His son would be moulded into an anti-capitalist.

Carefully crafted like a potter making a bowl from clay. Every step was logged and categorised. Filmed. Recorded for posterity, or that is what Viktor was told. All the groups he joined whilst going through his academic years, he was guided or steered to them. Manipulated by an unseen force, his father.

Titus hoped that the term '*Operation Hummingbird*' would become synonymous with the change in the balance of power. Family members over the years had approached Max expressing concern at the radical views and actions of Viktor. Max would either brush them off or hire an extremely well-paid doctor to alleviate their worries; by saying it was just a stage he was going through, and that he would grow out of it.

Over the years, Max had forged relationships with governments, or officials, and he was not averse to using them when the time needed. He sat in his office a top his headquarters in the capital and waited, sipping on a glass of scotch. He looked at the clock above the door opposite. Nine o'clock. He smiled and took another drink allowing the liquid to coat the inside of his throat with a warm glow. His intercom buzzed.

"The colonel for you, Herr Titus." Informed his assistant.

"Thank you." He manoeuvred his chair round so that he could see the large screen behind him and pressed a button on a remote. The screen flickered into life showing the head and shoulders of Macheyov, resplendent in his full colonel's uniform. "You are looking very smart this evening, colonel. Going to a fancy dress party?"

"A state luncheon with the president."

"Is he not attending the summit in Glasgow?" Asked Titus faking disappointment.

"No. He says it is a waste of his precious time instead; he wants all his senior officials to sit down with him and talk international policy."

"Both a pity and boring."

"Agreed. How is *'Operation Hummingbird'* proceeding?"

"As planned. My son and his minions should be boarding the bus around about now and they should be in position by one this afternoon at the latest."

"Good. The main speakers are due to arrive around three. When do you plan for our little demonstration to happen?"

"Colonel, please. I would like to keep some things a secret…" said Titus taking a sip from his drink. "Anyway, everyone likes a surprise. Don't they?" He started to laugh, more of a cackle than a full-blown laugh. Anyhow, it was infectious because Macheyov joined in.

Bishop's telephone chirped. She looked at the caller identification. It was an outside line. A number she did not recognise. Before she answered, she pressed another button on the main unit alerting her assistant to put a trace on the call and then she picked it up.

"Bishop."

"My name is Gregor Fuller."

"Mr. Fuller. Where are you? We are concerned for your safety. I can have a car at your location within minutes."

"I don't have much time." Said Fuller whispering, "I've managed to infiltrate the Wolf Pack. They're going to try something at the summit in Glasgow…." Fuller stopped suddenly then the line went dead.

"Hello…. Fuller…Hello…" Bishop looked over to her assistant through the window of her office. A shake of the assistant's head confirmed her fears.

Not on long enough to trace. "Damn it!" She cursed throwing the phone on to the cradle. She jumped to her feet and opened her office door.

"Listen up people!" She yelled, "that was Gregor Fuller on my outside line. He didn't say much except he suspects the Wolf Pack is planning something in Glasgow. I want everyone to start trawling through surveillance cameras, CCTV. Hell! Even your granny's mobile phone pictures! I want Viktor Titus and the Wolf Pack. Move people!"

It was as if someone had fired a starting pistol at the beginning of an athletics meeting. The once quiet office became a hive of activity instantly. The murmur of voices of people talking to each other, talking themselves through procedures on the monitors in front of them and looking through video footage.

Bishop's section was always a well-oiled machine. She knew that, but now they would be tested. She trusted them. They trusted her.

Meanwhile, Fuller climbed on to the bus, pulling his hood of his hoodie over his head. The small rucksack he had slung over his shoulder, hit another seated person on the knee, causing him to complain and asked him to watch what he was doing. Fuller apologised and sneaked a glancing look to the back of the vehicle where Titus was sitting lording it up. The incident had gone unnoticed, so Fuller found a seat, putting his rucksack on his knee.

He turned his head and looked out of the window, hoping that this Bishop person was high enough up the ladder of command to make a difference. Her name was third on the list that was mentioned in the covering letter his friend Foster had sent him.

Below Scott and someone called Jacob Fallon. Both were a bust. Scott's line was busy, and Fallon had not picked up either. He knew Scott was the head of the OSP but Fallon? Some wise guy Foster had pulled out of a hat. The bus lurched forward as it moved off.

Thirty minutes later, after Bishop had briefed all concerned, she was standing in front of a large monitor in the centre of her section's bull pen. Scott and Dexter were standing with her, reviewing what her section had found.

"We've got Titus leaving a student residence some thirty minutes ago on a bus." Began Lizzie.

"Where did you get the footage from?" Asked Scott.

"A security camera across the street belonging to the local private school sir."

"Do we have a positive I.D. on Titus?" Asked Bishop.

"Facial recognition is one hundred percent, boss." Replied Klein. Scott looked over at Bishop with a disapproving look on his face at the way Klein responded to her questioning, and the use of the word 'boss,' rather than 'madam.'

Bishop tilted her head slightly but said nothing. "I've managed to get the registration number of the bus and contacted the company. Once I'd jumped a few of their bureaucratic hurdles and mentioned this was a matter of national security, they produced the route and destination."

"Where?"

"Glasgow. Glasgow Green to be more precise."

"Jesus, Mary and Joseph!" Cursed Scott.

"Covering all your bases, huh?" Commented Bishop. Scott smiled nervously.

"According to our recent intel," added Dexter, "they've planned a massive demonstration against the summit and its kick-off point is Glasgow Green. Thousands of people are expected to attend. Men, women, and children. Even the leader of the opposition is due to speak at it."

"Anything to get their faces in front of the camera." Commented one of the other techs. Bishop looked over at him and gave him her famous 'death' stare. The man seemed to wither visibly in front of everyone turning a very strange colour.

"Right!" Ordered Scott. "I want this bus traced and tagged. Inform the locals that this bus is to be followed but no intervention unless authorised by me. Dexter, get onto K-12 and update him." Dexter nodded and moved to the side grabbing her mobile from her pocket. "Move people!"

"That's my line!" Protested Bishop with her tongue very firmly in her cheek. She walked over to Klein and stood behind her. "I want you to put a trace on Fuller's mobile and track it." Klein nodded and started typing.

"Got him boss." Klein said triumphantly.

"Good. If he keeps his phone on, we can track him."

"And if his battery dies, or he switches it off?" Asked Scott.

"Then we lose him, sir." Answered Klein before Bishop could. She looked over to her boss for reassurance, that she had not over stepped. Bishop nodded her approval.

16 – *Operation Hummingbird*

The presidential palace, or Kremlin, in Moscow, was an impressive looking building which had seen royalty come and go. Consisting of five palaces, four cathedrals, and the enclosing Kremlin Wall along with the Kremlin Towers. Within the complex is the Grand Kremlin Palace, which served as the royal residence of the emperor of Russia and now is the official residence of president of the Russian Federation. The building overlooks the Moskva River to the south, St. Basil's Cathedral and Red Square to the east, and Alexander Garden to the west.

The rise and fall of Communism, at least the vision of the founder members. There was a new Russia rising from the ashes, like the proverbial phoenix, dying and then being reborn in flame. Macheyov sat at one of the numerous tables laid out for the banquet in the main hall. He was just another face in a sea of faces and uniforms. The president had arrived, only minutes after he had arrived, and everyone was now tucking into their first courses. Something very light and unremarkable.

There was no menu, per-say, at these functions. You just sat down and consumed what was put in front of you. They tended to last for several courses before retiring to the large hall off to the left for the formal briefing. A passable glass of white wine sat in front of him. Not the vintage the president would wheel out for dignitaries but not something you would pour on your fish and chips either. Since the fall of the Berlin Wall, in November 1989, the economy had flourished with outside investment.

Business leaders had become multi-billionaires overnight and crime had become rampant too. Macheyov was about to reach for the wine glass when his mobile buzzed in his pocket. He took it out and looked at it. It was a message.

'OSP alerted to Hummingbird.' At the end of the message was an emoji of a phoenix. The message was from his mole in the OSP. Macheyov let out a curse in Russian that sounded more like a snake hissing than anything intelligible. It brought a look from the general sitting next to him.

"My pardon, comrade general. I have just received some destressing news." The general dismissed him with a wave of his hand. Once outside, in one of the many corridors, which branched off from the main hall, Macheyov called Max Titus. It rang once, before going to voice mail. The colonel cursed again and hung up.

His mind was now racing. Hummingbird had taken years in the planning. Titus had spent millions on it, leaning on him for technical support and funding, when the well, Titus had used, suddenly went dry at the beginning of the Noughties. Was this well constructed wall about to tumble down around him? He had to make plans in case the mortar started to weaken.

He turned and strode off towards the exit, faking making a call on his mobile when a subordinate tried to speak to him after first saluting. He put his mobile away as he came out into the courtyard where his car was waiting. His driver opened the rear left door and Macheyov climbed in. He made another couple of brief calls using the code phrase '*Lightning Bolt*' before hanging up. The car cleared the various checkpoints before heading off towards his flat in the city.

Fallon climbed onto the bus, heading to the former Airforce base. The trip would take him fifteen minutes. Dexter had briefed him on what was happening in Glasgow and had decided for a helicopter to take him there.

He got off and watched the bus pull away before crossing the road to the main gate of the base. A corporal came out of his hut ordering him to stop. Fallon reached into his pocket for his identification. The NCO (non-commissioned officer) raised his Heckler and Koch HK5 machine gun.

"Steady there, John Wayne!" Calmed Fallon. "I.D." The NCO lowered his weapon as he came forward and inspected Fallon's credentials.

"Sorry, sir." Apologised the soldier. "It's just the base has been put on high alert."

"Nothing to apologise for. Can you get someone to take me to my ride?" Fallon suggested putting away his identification.

"Oh yes. Of course, sir." The NCO disappeared for a moment into his box before emerging. "Someone will be here shortly." A jeep appeared from around the corner with a military policeman driving. He stopped beside Fallon.

"Major Fallon?" Asked the MP. Fallon nodded. "If you would get in, sir. Your chopper is waiting." Fallon climbed into the front passenger seat and with a screech of rubber, the jeep sped off towards a row of hangars. The conversation was muted.

Neither man spoke. The MP concentrating on his driving, while Fallon mulled over his mission details. The whir of a helicopter engine snapped him back to reality and looked over to see a Hughes MD-500 combat helicopter, with its rotors turning, ready for lift off. Dexter had pulled some strings.

The base had been taken over by the Army, six or so years previously, and only military or celebrity flights ever took off from here now. Fallon ran to the aircraft in a semi stoop. Opened the door and climbed aboard. Strapped himself in and adorned a headset complete with microphone. He gave the pilot a thumbs-up before giving the MP driver a wave, which was not returned. Instead, he got a salute which Fallon did return, and off into the wild blue yonder he went, momentarily leaving his stomach behind but he quickly recovered.

Fallon kept in constant contact with Dexter who fed him the latest updates, so he was up to speed when his helicopter touched down a few miles away from Glasgow Green. A squad of four unmarked cars greeted him as he exited the helicopter. Dexter ran forward and shook his hand, gesturing for him to follow her.

Talking was pointless, as it would be drowned out by the sound of the helicopter's engines. As soon as his passenger was clear, the pilot took off. The deafening roar of the engines quickly disappeared as did the helicopter. A woman wearing a Commander's police uniform stepped forward and offered Fallon a hand. Fallon shook it.

"Commander Farmer. Jacob Fallon." Introduced Dexter as the threesome walked towards the awaiting cars.

"Major Fallon."

"Commander Farmer."

"Commander Gillian Farmer is head of the Anti-Terrorism Unit." Said Dexter as they got into the dark coloured saloon.

Fallon and Farmer in the rear whilst Dexter sat in the front passenger seat. Once everyone had secured their seat belts, the cars sped off, the blue lights hidden behind the front grill, flashing rhythmically on and off. A point car led the way with Fallon, Farmer, and Dexter in the middle whilst another car, containing Special Branch officers slotted in at the rear.

"Last fix had the target entering the city limits." Informed Dexter.

"Unmarked units are following at a safe distance. Ready to intercept on my command." Added Farmer.

"Good. Do we have any Intel about what they're planning?" Asked Fallon.

"Nothing concrete. Fuller's last message was just that the Wolf Pack were planning something to do with the conference."

"Has security been stepped up?"

"Nothing more than normal for this type of event. Your superiors made it quite clear that if we increase our presence, then we could scare them off, and lose them forever." Fallon could tell Farmer was unhappy with this arrangement, but she followed orders as did he. So, they were both in the same boat, waiting to see what the target's next move was going to be.

"We have armed officers at all the strategic points. Entrances and exits are all covered, as well as any vantage point deemed significant."

"Good. Where are we going now?"

"Thought we might take a look at the Green from a safe distance." Replied Farmer.

"Okay."

The convoy whizzed through the traffic. The flashing blue lights helped, as did the several officers on motorbikes, that magically appeared at the junctions along the way. Each officer waved the cars through, before restarting the flow of traffic, much to the annoyance of several motorists, who made their displeasure known, by honking their horns. The cars turned into a car park a few miles from the Green; the police having commandeered the area as a mobile command centre.

A large trailer, with writing on the side that broadcast this to anyone who wished to know, took centre stage. A taped cordon had been thrown around the trailer. A policeman on the edge of the cordon stopped the cars and asked for identification. Upon receiving confirmation, he waved them through.

Farmer was the first to get out and walk up the steps into the trailer. Fallon and Dexter followed. Inside was a mass of surveillance equipment. Television monitors streaming live feed. Each monitor was manned by a uniformed officer who constantly scanned the pictures.

"We're tied into everything from CCTV, traffic cameras and even television feeds. Facial recognition software is sifting through all the images, trying to get a fix on the target. We have airborne units circling the sky above the venue and mobile units on constant patrol." Said Farmer with some measure of pride. Both Fallon and Dexter were impressed. "A fly couldn't get through without alerting someone."

"What about at the venue?" Asked Dexter.

"Armed officers are patrolling the perimeter; security staff search everyone who goes in and out."

"Won't this tip our hand to the targets?" Asked a worried Dexter.

"No. The people of Glasgow are used to this level of security for this type of event. Especially after the recent terror attacks both here and abroad." Came the reply.

"Ma'am." An officer walked over to Farmer and handed her a piece of paper.

"Damn it!" Farmer swore.

"What is it?" Asked Fallon.

"They've decided to have an assembly point outside the city before marching on the Green for the speeches."

"Do we know where this is?" Asked Fallon moving over to one of the monitors.

"A field the organisers have rented. They've installed porta-loos and even concession stands."

"The groups not going to hit Glasgow Green." Said Dexter having a Eureka moment.

"Come again." Asked a puzzled Farmer.

"Where can you cause the most damage? Think about it!"

"When people are assembling, they will be disorganised and off guard." Answered Fallon.

"Exactly!"

17 – *Sacrificial Lamb*

The bus pulled into one of the many bays set aside for such vehicles. One of the men near the front, Robert, stood up and started chanting racist slogans to rile up the group. Some joined in but others remained silent, walking passed him instead and retrieving their placards from underneath the bus.

The Werner twins reached in and pulled out their hold-all looking up at Titus who was watching from the window above. He nodded. They nodded before heading towards one of the large areas set aside for toilets. There was a smallish building, the size of a porta-cabin, was where the security staff had their uniforms, and equipment. Klaus Werner tried the door.

Unsurprisingly, it was locked. He took out a screwdriver and forced the lock. The two men disappeared inside closing the door behind them. Once safely inside, Otto opened the bag, to reveal a bomb, consisting of blocks of C4 explosive, a detonator, a mobile phone, and a battery to power a small clock, insurance as Viktor had referred to it.

Otto looked at his watch and then texted Titus for instructions. Straight away, Titus messaged back telling him to set the back-up timer for four hours, enough time for them to get away. He did as he was told, before they both grabbed a small Ingram machine pistol and a couple of extra clips from the hold-all before zipping it back up.

The two men appeared from the cabin resplendent in their new security uniforms that they had just liberated. Proceeding to manhandle the hold-all towards a stationary ice-cream van. Klaus took a set of keys from his trouser pocket and unlocked the back of the van before helping his brother lift the bag into the back. They made sure it was secure before locking it down and leaving, mingling with the assembling crowd. The plan was coming together nicely.

At the height of the rally, thousands of people will be assembling to march on Glasgow Green, surrounding the ice-cream van oblivious to its deadly contents, and Viktor was not talking about the ice-cream. He allowed himself a cruel satisfied smile as he text a number.

"The hummingbird has learned to fly."

Miles away, Max Titus received a text that made his heart fly with indescribable pleasure. "The hummingbird has learned to fly." He relayed the message on to Macheyov who, unlike his co-conspirator, moved uneasily in his chair. A bead of sweat trickled down the side of his left temple. He took out a handkerchief from the breast pocket of his uniform and mopped his brow.

Suddenly feeling a mixture of emotions – elation at the fact the plan had begun and fear at what the repercussions would be.

"Are you alright, comrade colonel?" Asked a concerned subordinate who just happened to be walking past Macheyov as he was taking some air.

"Da. Thank you for your concern, lieutenant."

The lieutenant saluted and continued upon his way. Macheyov saluted back, continuing his walk along the promenade, flanked as always, by his security detail and his car, both of which supported a reasonable distance.

Fuller watched from across the field as the Werner twins made their way through security thanks to their newly acquired uniforms. He videoed them with his mobile, having to hold it in both hands, to compensate for them shaking, stopping recording when they went out of sight.

His next target was Viktor. It took him a few minutes to find him but when he did, he was walking away from the field. Fuller found this odd. His henchmen were still here. Why would he be leaving? He decided to follow.

"We've got him!" Yelled one of the officers, manning the surveillance monitors in the trailer. Farmer, Fallon, and Dexter crowded around.

"Where?" Asked Farmer.

"There, ma'am." Said the officer pointing to the screen. "Heading away from the field."

"Looks like he's got a shadow." Fallon pointed out pointing to a figure in close pursuit.

"That must be Fuller. The bloody idiot!" Cursed Farmer. "He's going to ruin everything!"

She walked over to another officer. "Alert all units in the area to close in and apprehend Viktor Titus and Gregor Fuller."

"Yes, ma'am."

"I know this wasn't what the OSP wanted...." Began Farmer turning back to the agents but was greeted by an open door. A squeal of tyres told her where Fallon and Dexter had gone. "Bloody hell!" She turned back to the communications officer. "Inform all units that we have undercover operatives in the area. Circulate pictures of Fallon and Dexter, so that someone with an itchy trigger finger doesn't shoot them by mistake."

The black Chevrolet Impala, driven by Fallon, hurtled towards the last known position of Titus and Fuller. Deciding to not go quietly, Fallon had the lights flashing and the sirens blaring.

"Amazing how the traffic gets out of the way when you're in a hurry." He commented as he threw the car around a corner.

"Must get this for the old Aston when I get back. Would let me pop out for a curry during the intermission of the match and get back in time for the second half."

With its headlights and grill lights flashing, the saloon screamed to a halt outside a building site, according to the police radio chatter, this was the last place Titus and Fuller had been spotted. The car doors flew open, and the two operatives tumbled out.

Fallon with his Walther already drawn and Dexter pulling back the slide on her Walther. They looked at each other, as if telepathically transferring their plan of attack to each other, before sprinting off in opposite directions.

The site had been closed by the authorities, as a security precaution, so it was deserted apart from the two operatives and hopefully, their targets. As they bailed on Farmer, Fallon had picked up two earwig communication devices. He had kept one for himself and handed the other to Dexter.

"Dex?"

"Jake."

"Anything?"

"Nothing. Heading towards the staff caravans."

"Copy. Heading towards the building."

"Copy."

Dexter methodically checked the first small caravan. The door was locked. No sign of life. She held her pistol in both hands, extending her arms as she rounded the corner. Nothing. She edged her way forward, watching her footfall, stopping at the next caravan. Larger than the earlier one. Putting her back against the wagon, she tried the door. It moved.

She opened it slowly and counted to ten before jumping in front of the doorway, arms extended, breathing hard, adrenaline coursing through her veins. She was running on a mixture of her training and instinct. Ears straining for the slightest sound. Pupils wide looking for any sign of movement. She popped her head into the caravan, looking to one side then the next in a sharp meerkat like motion. When she looked to the left, something moved.

"I'm armed. Come out with your hands raised above your head!" She ordered. Nothing. She stepped up into the caravan facing the direction of the movement.

"Last warning." She cocked her weapon.

The sound of scratching off to the right. There was a door. She just got to it, about to open it, when it exploded into pieces, as Titus ran through it and her, sending

Dexter spiralling to the floor. Her gun flew from her hands across the floor and went under a small table. Titus looked at her, then at the weapon and back at her. Dexter did the same.

"Dex.... Dex..." It was Fallon shouting in her ear. The momentary distraction was time enough for Titus, who had decided that cowardice was the safest choice, he legged it out of the caravan. "Dex..."

"I'm here!" She yelled getting slowly to her feet, still feeling the effects of the collision. Winded, she reached down and picked up the Walther.

"Are you okay?"

"I had him!" She cursed.

"Fuller?"

"No. Titus."

"What happened?"

"He jumped me and got away. He's somewhere in the site. Watch yourself."

"Copy."

Fallon was at the base of the construction. Looked like a massive prehistoric animal whose bones had been picked clean by a long-deceased predator. After what had just happened to Dexter, he was on high alert.

Scanning his surroundings with ever step. He walked cautiously around the corner and came face to face with both Fuller and Titus, the latter looking down the barrel of an automatic held by the former.

"Why did you have my father killed?" Asked Fuller.

"It wasn't me."

"You lie! It might have been one of your cronies who did it, but you ordered it!" Yelled Fuller tears stinging his eyes.

"It wasn't me." Repeated Viktor.

"But you know who did."

Viktor smiled a knowing smile which escalated the tension. Fuller took a couple of steps forward grabbing his weapon with both hands, his hands trembling.

"You won't shoot. You don't have the guts. You're weak…" Titus taunted.

"He might not but I will." Interjected Fallon walking out from the shadows, the Walther aimed at Titus' head. "Go ahead. Give me a reason."

"Who are you?" Asked a distraught Fuller.

"The name's Fallon. I work for the Office of Special Projects."

"Stay out of this." Pleaded Fuller. "This has nothing to do with you!"

"Sorry, Gregor, I can't." Replied Fallon.

"Pleassseee!" Fuller begged.

"This asshole has something bigger planned, and I need to know what it is."

Viktor laughed.

"Listen, dickhead." Hissed Fallon, "you can walk outta here with me, and spend the rest of your miserable life in prison, or I can walk away, and let him kill you. Your choice."

Viktor laughed again and pulled out his mobile phone, holding it at arms-length for all to see. Dexter came running around into view, her automatic also trained on Titus.

"Wolf...." Viktor started to shout but was stopped as bullets from both Dexter's automatic and Fallon's Walther cut him down before he could either continue or press any buttons. Dexter walked slowly across, weapon still trained and knelt to check for signs of life. She shook her head.

"You could say, his party didn't end with a bang." Fallon looked down at Dexter, who smiled before he holstered his weapon and walked over to Fuller, putting his hand on top of the automatic.

"It's over Gregor. You can give me the weapon now." Fallon whispered calmly. Fuller nodded slowly, releasing the gun. Fallon took it and put it in his pocket, patting Fuller on the shoulder, signifying he had done the right thing.

"I guess we'll never know what he had planned." Said Dexter, as her comment was almost drowned out by the wail of sirens, as the Police arrived, accompanied by a peeved Farmer.

"Wait a minute!" Corrected Fuller, as he finally came out of the haze that had silenced him. "I've got this." He took out his mobile and brought up the mobile footage of the Werner twins. Unknown to Fuller, he had actually caught them coming out of the back of the ice-cream truck in their uniforms.

Farmer grabbed the phone and passed it to one of her technicians, who ran back to the car, popped the boot, and pulled out a laptop. He took out a lead from his pocket, connecting one end to the computer and the other to Fuller's phone. A few key presses later, and he had managed to isolate a decent picture of the twins. He looked over to Farmer, who nodded. The technician pressed a button and instantly circulated the picture.

Klaus and his brother had made their way across the site and were approaching an ice cream van. It was locked and apart from the two of them, no one else was around. Klaus' hand went into his overalls and pulled out a set of keys. The sight of which made his brother smile.

The largest key on the ring was inserted into the door on the driver's side and turned. Click and the door was unlocked. Klaus pulled it open and climbed inside, turning to his brother, who handed him the large bag he had been carrying.

Klaus took it and pulled it inside, then his brother followed, bringing up the rear. The door of the van closing behind them. The duo moved through a small opening between the seats to the back of the van where all the merchandise was stored in either refrigerated tubs that went from waist height down to the floor or up on shelves that had been bolted to the inside of the vehicle.

Klaus, staying in a crouched position to avoid detection, pulled the bag along the linoleum covered floor. It slid easily towards him. He reached over, grasped the large metal toggle that was attached to the zip and pulled it towards him exposing the contents for the first time.

Blocks of what looked like modelling clay to the untrained eye were nestled amongst an entanglement of different coloured wires. A large clock sat off to the left being cuddled by a mobile phone, neither of which was active.

The sight of this made both brothers smile contentedly, like children on Christmas day as they unwrap a present, they had always wanted.

Klaus stopped for a moment and unzipped his top, reached inside and pulled out an automatic weapon, a Uzi submachine gun, placing it down beside him on the floor. He looked across at Otto, who, slow to take up the hint, eventually caught up and copied his brother. They were now ready for anything.

"What do we do now?" Asked Otto.

"We are waiting until we have received more orders." Answered Klaus, glancing at his watch. *Wait until they receive further orders*, Klaus repeated to himself in his head. Viktor was the man in charge, but he was late and this worried the German, although he tried his best to hide this from his brother.

"Can I see it again?" Pleaded Otto, asking to see the bomb one final time. Klaus nodded and shuffled back a few metres to allow his sibling a better view.

Otto raised himself up from a crouch until his head was visible through the glass window covering the opening in the side of the van where the contents were distributed to the awaiting customers.

As luck would have it, two firearms officers from the anti-terrorist unit passed the van as they were conducting a sweep of the area looking for the twins.

One of them noticed Otto's head peaking above the shelf and he checked the picture he had that they had received before setting out. His hand shot up to the radio on his chest, a thumb pressing down on the send button and within minutes, the van was surrounded by armed officers, all keeping a safe distance in case the occupants wanted to go out in a blaze of glory.

"This is inspector Stephen Clark. I am addressing the occupants of the vehicle in front of me. Come out with your arms above your heads or we will open fire!" Instructed an officer through a loud hailer. The men outside waited. "If you're armed, throw your weapons out first and then alight the vehicle with your hands..." began Clark but he was sent diving for cover as a hail of automatic fire came from the van.

"Long live the wolf pack!" Screamed a voice from within the van causing Clark to shake his head reluctantly. He turned to the officer on his right and nodded.

"Open fire!" Yelled the officer. From a distance, it sounded like a choir of angry woodpeckers hammering out their version of a heavy metal classic but to the Werner's within the van, the metal was far more deadly. Their bodies gyrating and shaking as multiple rounds pierced their bodies. If they had entered a breakdancing competition in the 1980s, they would have surely won first place.

The rounds from the police officers machine guns peppered the vans, it to joining in with the Werners as the impact of the onslaught made the vehicle bounce up and down, turning the once pristine mode of transport into something like either a large chunk of Swiss cheese or the remnants left over from a feasting frenzy from a swarm of moths.

After what seemed like forever, the cease fire order was shouted. Clark signalled for a couple of officers to approach the van, which they did cautiously, whilst the others gave them cover. The one in the lead crouched down below the rear door, reached up and tried the handle.

It was unlocked.

A stray bullet from the attack had smashed the lock to smithereens. He looked back at his colleague, who slowly raised his machine gun, and the man on the door pulled it open.

Silence.

He got slowly to his feet and looked inside. Devastation met his eyes. A mosaic of death. Blood mixed with mint choc-chip. Vanilla became chunky with flesh and brain matter. The sight was both grotesque and beautiful in equal measures.

Colourful and horrific. Street art at its most savage would be how one of the crime scene technicians would later go on to describe it to a reporter when pressed on what he had seen that day. The corpses lay sprawled on the ground. The furthest away one was spread eagled over a duffel bag or something similar.

The officer looked back at the others, raised his first two fingers of his right hand in the air then change to his thumb, inverting it downwards, signalling that the two occupants were both dead. He turned and started to walk back from the van, his companion joining him.

"What a bloody mess." The first officer whispered to his colleague. "And for what?" His companion shrugged.

Three hours later, Farmer sat opposite the two operatives in her office.

"Well, that almost ended up in a major f...." Her telephone rang. "Commander Farmer.... Yes minister... Yes, we did dodge the proverbial bullet.... Yes minister... You're welcome.... Thank you and goodbye." Fallon and Dexter looked across at her with smug looks on their faces. "That was the home secretary."

"Really? And what did she want?" Asked Fallon.

"Okay. Cut that shit out!" Farmer finally snapped.

"Cut what out, commander?" Fallon asked looking at Dexter then back at Farmer.

"That smug *'we've saved the day'* look you both have on your faces!"

"Us?" Said Fallon sarcastically pointing to the two of them. Dexter shook her head, pretending not to have a clue what the commander was referring to.

"Anyway, the firearms unit caught up with the Werner twins, who decided it was better to die in a hail of bullets than to surrender."

"And the bomb?"

"A crude explosive device that a six-year-old could have defused, according to the disposal people, but they didn't have time to arm it."

"Strange. Why would such a hi-tech group use such a crude device?" Puzzled Fallon.

"Maybe the bomb wasn't their mission." Suggested Dexter. "Maybe there was a second more important mission that the Wolf Pack didn't know about."

"You mean they were patsies?" Said Farmer.

"Maybe. Part of a larger more complex plan."

"Letting the Wolf Pack take the blame for the bombing whilst someone else benefits." Said Fallon.

"Exactly."

18 – *Business as Usual*

After several hours of de-briefing back at headquarters, both Fallon and Dexter stood at attention in front of Scott. For both, the situation felt strangely familiar. Scott looked over the after-action report given by both operatives. He had already had to suffer an earful from commander Farmer, who was still upset by the two of them riding off to fight the bad guys without back-up. Scott chewed down on the tip of his pipe, a sign to his operatives that he was far from happy.

"Wanton destruction of property and more to the point, OSP equipment…"

"If you're referring to the Aston and the Mustang…" Began Fallon.

"Did I ask you to speak, K-12?"

"No sir." *Welcome back to the headmaster's study.* Fallon thought as he fidgeted from one foot to the other, looking up to the ceiling rather than trade glances with his superior.

"On a positive note, we stopped a major attack that could have cost thousands of lives, never mind the political fallout."

"At least there's a positive, sir." Added Dexter. Scott glared at her.

"Two operatives who should be suspended.... No! Fired!"

"But sir!" Both operatives protested in stereo.

"Let me finish." Snapped Scott holding a hand up. "It seems that you both have a guardian angel in the government. The Home Secretary has asked me to pass on her congratulations, and also her thanks for a successful mission."

"She has also instructed me to add a commendation to both your files. It would seem you've both dodged a bullet. If I had my way, you'd be both out on your ears, but I've been overruled..."

Both operatives beamed with pride.

"Now, get out!" The smile disappeared as they made a hasty exit.

Somewhere in a dingy one bedroomed flat, a mobile flashed and played the theme from 'The Godfather.' A woman walked over to where the phone sat and picked it up from the table, walked across to the small window, as she answered. Macheyov's voice spoke.

"The phoenix has died."

"But it will arise anew, from the ashes." Came the response.

"The mission was a success?" Macheyov asked.

"Yes. OSP are now looking over their shoulders delving into a larger plot."

"Good. Do they suspect you?"

"No."

"Good. Until the next time, my little phoenix."

"Goodbye, papa." The woman hung up and returned to the bedroom where Igor Marinko lay there naked under a flimsy sheet. She walked slowly over to the bed, dropping her see-through gown on the floor as she approached showing a tattoo of the fiery bird of legend on her left buttock, a reminder from her student days.

Marinko smiled as the woman climbed on top of the covers, slithering her way across to him. "He still has no clue." She said before they kissed.

"More tea, Amy?" Asked Molly, reaching for a large teapot with flowers on it.

"Just a smidge." Lady Amy Spence replied as she nibbled down on a triangle of cucumber and water cress sandwich.

"I'd like to thank you again, for coming to my son's rescue, after this frightful affair." A grateful Molly said as she handed Lady Amy her cup on a saucer.

"No problem, Molls." Replied Lady Amy, her accent dropping slightly. "Us prep schoolgirls must stick together you know."

"Another sandwich or a scone, perhaps?" Molly asked picking up a plate weighed down by such delights.

The conference would go ahead without a hitch. World leaders would go through the political motions of pledging this and that, in public, but secretly making deals behind closed doors. A young Swedish activist, Greta Thunberg, would make a passionate plea to the

World, both outside to the throng of demonstrators and inside, to the suits, the men in power.

The conference would feature in news reports for a few days and then fade into memory being replaced by something more important, a dog being rescued, in a once Eastern Bloc country, from a sewage drain by mud caked firefighters.

A picture was flashed around the globe showing the animal in his relieved owner's arms.

Meanwhile, a couple of days later, sitting in his office, a top his headquarters, Maximillian Titus sipped on a drink. You would think he would be beside himself with grief after the death of his son, but on the contrary, he was pleased with himself. He gave a brief toast to his deceased son, but that was all the recognition the youth received. Love was not in the Titus vocabulary.

There was no place in his icy heart for such a useless and unwarranted emotion. His son had served his purpose. His right index finger and thumb reached over to the ring on his left ring finger and twiddled it, spinning it round and around. It was gold with a black circle with two numbers embossed in the middle. Seven and eight. He stood up and raised his glass once more, before shouting to an empty room:

"Setenta y Ocho!"

Fallon will Return...

About Robyn Smythe

R obyn Smythe is a Scottish writer. Born in the 60's in Fife, he was educated at Madras College secondary school where he wrote his first full length story. More than three decades later, after a varied working life that has involved being a lifeguard and Post Office clerk, he finally found time to write Fallon, his debut novel. He is married with two daughters.

Other Titles by Robyn Smythe

Children's Fiction

The Animal Tea Party

Fudge – A Short Tail of Tooth and Claw

Claws and Paws

Arthur – The Aardvark

Adult Fiction

Fallon – Non Est Optio Defectum

Fallon 2 – Family Above All

Fallon 3 – The Gathering Storm

A Ghost of a Man

Coming Soon

Animal Mayhem